Like Falling from an Airplane

Jim Antonini

Enjoy!

Pump Fake Press—Morgantown, WV
ISBN: 978-0-578-36646-3
Library of Congress Control Number: pending
Title: *Like Falling from an Airplane*
Author: Jim Antonini
Digital distribution | 2022
Paperback | 2022

Cover artwork by Chris Antonini

Dedication

To fireflies, tequila, a jukebox, and time

About the Author

Jim Antonini resides in Morgantown, WV. *Like Falling from an Airplane* is his second published novel.

His first book 'Bullets for Silverware' was a finalist for the Appodlachia 2020 Best Appalachian Book of the Year.

What others have said:

"...the characters were real... like I knew them personally... the prose itself was the real prize- gritty, sympathetic... READ THIS BOOK!" - Amazon review - 07/07/2020

"...chills, titillates, and above all entertains...the scenes roll out smoothly, and it is easy to imagine this story as film noir...has a Hitchcockian flavor..." - Independent Book Review - 07/28/2020

"...feels fast-paced, hard-boiled, and edgy..." - BookTrib - 05/05/2021

Please visit: www.jim-antonini.squarespace.com

Chapter One
Don't You Believe in Love at First Sight?

Jonathan knew it was a mistake to leave the Tenderloin neighborhood near downtown San Francisco where he lived. As he circled the narrow and hilly streets of North Beach, he searched for a parking spot. He rarely left his neighborhood. He didn't have to. The gritty Tenderloin had all he could ever want or need. It had been a good place to hide over the years. But what the hell. He had a car for the day, a little cash, and he knew a woman in North Beach he'd been wanting to see.

William, his brother, was getting married in the coming days, and his folks who he rarely saw, wanted Jonathan to get cleaned up. So, they gave him $300 for a new suit and haircut. His mother also loaned him her vintage, baby-blue Volkswagen bug, so he could get around. The young woman in North Beach was good at cutting hair, among other things.

The old Volkswagen staggered and sputtered on the steep hills as Jonathan overworked an unfamiliar clutch while searching for a parking spot. He looked out of place with a bouquet of daises on the dashboard. His rough appearance- long, wild hair and arms covered in tattoos, clashed with the car's retro, soft leather interior. He tapped his hands and sang along to the Jimi Hendrix song, *"Crosstown Traffic"*, that loudly rattled from the radio.

Growing more frustrated, Jonathan expertly squeezed the Volkswagen into a tight space on top of Chestnut Street. He got out of the car and studied his park job. The car was tightly edged against a fire hydrant. He checked his watch and looked around, then shrugged. Before leaving the car, he stood upon the hill overlooking the San Francisco Bay and watched the orange glow of sunset give way to the cold and dark, burgundy sky at dusk.

In her cramped studio apartment, Susan straddled Jonathan's legs as she cut the hair on one side of his head. With his knee, he rubbed between her legs.

"Jonathan. Cut it out," she begged him and chuckled at the same time as she struggled to cut his long, shaggy hair. "Stop it."

Shirtless with a towel over his shoulders, he sat facing her on a kitchen chair. He was thin but muscular, with faded tattoos decorating his arms and back.

"Do you want me to cut your hair or not?"

Grinning, he reached for the scissors. She tried to pull them away.

"Jonathan."

He grabbed the scissors from her hand and tossed them on
a table. Only one side of his hair had been cut. He stood, took her in his arms, and brushed away the dirty blonde hair that had fallen over her face. She resisted at first, then accepted his advance as he nibbled her ear lobe.

"I knew I shouldn't have let you come over," she giggled.

They fell back against a wall embraced in a heated kiss. As he worked to unbutton her blouse, a loud noise from outside briefly distracted them. Susan tried to glance out the window, but Jonathan wouldn't allow her. Another loud bang followed.

"Jonathan ..." she mumbled, smothered in his arms.

The non-stop beep of a backing truck sounded. Susan craned her neck and peered out a window.

"Jonathan. Your car!"

He glanced out the window. The Volkswagen was hitched to a tow truck. He threw open the window.

"Hey! Stop! That's my mom's car!"

Jonathan, bare-chested and in nothing but jeans and cowboy boots, dashed after the tow truck as it slowly pulled the car away. The tow truck driver reached his meaty arm out the driver's side window and saluted Jonathan with a raised middle finger.

"Hey. Hey. Wait. Stop. Dammit."

Jonathan ran faster, chasing the tow truck for almost a block. Angry as the truck pulled further away, he reached down and picked up a large piece of gravel, heaving it as far as he could in the direction of the truck. Well off its target, the rock bounced off the pavement and rolled harmlessly under a parked car as the tow truck drove away. Out of breath, Jonathan kicked at the ground, shook his head, and spat. He leaned forward and placed his hands on his knees, trying to catch his breath.

Night had quietly fallen, and the fog had drifted in off the bay. As Jonathan stared up to the steep hill that led back to Susan's place, a black Pruis hybrid suddenly pulled to a stop next to him and doubled parked.

A young woman hopped out, left the car running, and hurried into a nearby convenience store. Jonathan stared at the car a moment and then glanced around a few times. Without much thought, he jumped in the car and peeled away as the girl exited the store.

"Hey," She called, dropping a pack of cigarettes.

Weaving around cars, Jonathan drove the stolen Prius at dangerously high speeds on the Bayshore freeway that circled the city. The compact car squealed around turn after turn of the winding and hilly bypass road as he continued the joyride for several miles away from downtown. Still shirtless, Jonathan pulled off a random exit, accelerated the Prius, and boldly passed another car on a double-lined section of the road of some city suburb he's never been. Laughing out loud, he slammed the gas pedal to the floor as he came upon a straightaway. The car zoomed up and over a hill in the road. As the car crested the hill, it momentarily left the surface of the road.

"Yeee-owwww!" He screamed, sticking his head out the window.

Holding tightly to the steering wheel, Jonathan let out another yell as the car smashed down on the road with a loud crash. Sparks, glass, and hubcaps flew. With flapping flat tires, he turned into a parking lot. White smoke poured from the engine as the car chugged and stalled to a stop. He tried the ignition a few times, but the Prius wouldn't start. He glanced around to see where he had ended up. The car had broken down in the parking lot of a strip club located in a neighborhood outside of the city.

"Fate," he mumbled, staring up to the club's flashing neon sign.

He searched the inside of the car, opened the glove box, and went through it, tossing aside assorted papers and documents. He glanced in the back seat and grabbed a duffel bag. He rummaged through it. The bag contained mostly personal, work-out gear. He tossed them aside, except for a pink T-shirt that he slung over his bare shoulder and a pink razor he slipped in his pants' pocket before getting out of the car.

At the entrance to the club, he pulled on the pink shirt. It read in bold black capital letters, "*Princess*". The shirt was very tight on him. He patted at his half-cut hair and studied the reflection of his ragged appearance in the shaded glass of the door at the entrance.

He entered. The music was blistering loud. Several nude women of different ages and body shapes danced on the bar and on assorted tables arranged around the club. Nodding his head and checking out the scene, he took a seat at an empty table. A young stripper, who wore a see-through lace top over a brightly colored bikini, quickly brought him a beer and joined him at the table, showing off her biggest and best smile.

"Are you lonely tonight?" she playfully asked.

"You were reading my mind."

"Is there anything I can do about it?"

"You tell me?" he asked, studying her closely as he took a drink of beer.

"How far are you willin' to go?"

"Ah, I've been known to go pretty far."

"I don't come cheap."

"What's five bucks get me?"

"A smile, maybe some small talk."

"How 'bout 50?"

"I'll take you to the back for a little surprise," she grinned.

"I got some weed in my pocket," he said. "I hate smoking alone." She shrugged as he paused. "And $300."

"Follow me," she said, standing and taking his hand.

Jonathan and the stripper fervidly made out in a back seat of an old Buick in a side parking lot. Nearly smothering her, he tugged at her bikini bottom as she frantically worked to unzip his jeans. Pulling more of her lean body underneath him, he slobbered her perfumed neck and face with wet kisses as he dug his hand deeper between her thighs. Moaning in delight, or more likely at the prospect of $300, she stretched her long, slender legs up above their tangled bodies. Her feet pressed against the ceiling inside the car.

"Jesus, you *are* lonely," she gasped, nearly out of breath.

"You have no idea," he groaned into her ear.

"What about the weed?"

Suddenly, there was a tapping on the window. Jonathan and the stripper initially ignored it. The tapping continued but louder. A flash of light shined in the window. Jonathan turned to the light.

"Beat it, asshole," he grumbled as more light flooded the back seat of the car.

Jonathan and the stripper were ordered to get out of the car. Two policemen aimed flashlights at them as they stood outside of the Buick. Jonathan's pants were unbuttoned and unzipped. The "*Princess*" T-shirt he wore was stretched and turned sideways across his chest and back. The cops leered at the stripper. Nearly half-naked, she tried to cover herself with bent arms, hiding her face in one her of hands.

"She's my girlfriend."

"What's her name?" one of the cops asked.

"Huh?"

"What's her name?"

Jonathan glanced at the stripper as if looking for a clue. She shrugged. He looked back to the cops.

"Snooki?"

"All right, funny guy."

The cops roughly grabbed the back of Jonathan's shirt, turned him around as he struggled with them, and slammed him against the car. They handcuffed him before eventually finding a blanket to cover the stripper and handcuffing her.

"Hey. Wait. Stop," Jonathan hollered. "Jesus. We just met. We had no time for introductions."

Jonathan continued to struggle with the cops as they stuffed him in the back of their cruiser.

"You just ruined our first date. I hope you're happy."

Jonathan jerked back in the seat and slammed his feet on the floor of the squad car.

"Don't you believe in love at first sight?"

7

Chapter Two
Relax, Buddy, I'm Not the One Marrying Your
Daughter.

In a doctor's office examination room, a little girl, being held by her mother, screamed in pain. With long tweezers, William gently pulled a long splinter from the girl's foot. After removing the splinter, he lightly dabbed at the bloody spot on the foot with an antiseptic solution and a piece of gauze before applying a cartoon-covered bandage.

"There you go. No more pain."

The girl stopped crying. William wiped away the tears that hung on her cheeks.

"All better?"

The girl nodded, trying her best to smile. William handed her a lollipop.

"Thank you, Dr. Bill," the girl's mother smiled. "You're always there for us."

"Now keep her off that foot for a few days."

The mother nodded as William hugged the girl. After the girl and her mother left the examination room, a nurse entered.

"Katherine's outside."

William opened the door. Katherine, a tall, striking, and tanned brunette, smiled and entered as the nurse left the room. William and Katherine embraced and kissed.

"I miss you, baby," he said.

"Sneak away for lunch?"

"Wish I could," he shook his head, "but the waiting room's full. You know my motto, 'Patients …'"

"*Patients First*, I know," she interrupted.

"One more day, then I'm free," he promised. "I can't wait for the wedding."

"It'll be the happiest day of my life."

"How are you so sure?"

"Because I will finally have you all to myself," she said. "No patients. No clinics. No board meetings. No all-day golf outings."

The nurse opened the door and poked her head into the room.

"Dr. Bill?"

"OK. OK. Get the next one."

William turned to Katherine and pecked her on the cheek.

"See you tonight?" she asked.

"It'll be another late one. Better get dinner without me."

"Wake me when you get in."

"I will. We'll continue our family planning activities."

They kissed.

"I love you, baby," she said.

"I love you, too."

The nurse returned with a young patient and his mother as Katherine left the room.

"Timmy, my man."

"Hey, Dr. Bill."

"Tell me what's going on, buddy."

Locked in a dingy holding cell at the county jail on Bryant Street in downtown San Francisco, Jonathan violently rattled the bars of the cell.

"Hey. Hey. Let me outta here," Jonathan called out as the correctional officer sitting at a desk near the cell ignored him. "My brother's getting married. I need to be there. Hey."

Disinterested, the officer continued to stare at a newspaper and wouldn't look up. Jonathan angrily stomped on the foot pedal of the cell's toilet, causing it to repeatedly flush. The officer finally glanced up, shook his head, and pressed a button. The bars to the neighboring cell opened. An ugly, obese inmate with greasy hair and black rotten teeth entered Jonathan's cell. Jonathan turned and peeked over his shoulder. The hulking inmate towered over him. Jonathan glanced to the desk officer, then to the inmate in his cell, before stomping one last time on the toilet's foot pedal. The officer nodded, and the inmate cocked his arm. Before Jonathan could react, he was dropped to the floor by the hard punch from a gigantic left hand, knocked out cold.

On a lush lawn that rolled for several acres behind a stately brownstone church in North Beach, a long table was elegantly decorated with white candles and colorful arrangements of tulips, lilies, and hydrangeas. Delectable plates of imported cheeses and Italian meats, Dungeness crab, grilled vegetables, and steaks along with numerous expensive bottles of local cabernets and chardonnays covered the table. Katherine, her parents, and a few others were seated with William and his father, Ray. No one had eaten.

The bottles of wine remained corked. Instead, they waited. William's mother, Sandra, stood at the entrance of the church.

"What is your mother doing?" Katherine politely asked William.

"Waiting for Jonathan," Ray answered.

"I knew we shouldn't have invited him," William snapped.

With a black eye, bruised cheek, and several ink-stained fingers, Jonathan stood at the front desk of the county jail and signed a form. A correctional officer dumped out a large envelope that held Jonathan's personal items. The envelope contained several loose cigarettes, a bar napkin with a phone number and a dirty joke written on it, a condom, and the pink razor.

"You sure there wasn't any cash on me when I came in here?" Jonathan asked. "Say $300 or so?"

The officer shrugged as Jonathan slowly stuffed the items in his pockets. He then brushed at the pink T-shirt he wore and stared up at the officer who studied him with a puzzled gaze. Jonathan smirked and held up the pink razor before putting it in his pocket.

"What's with all the pink?" the officer asked.

"It's the new black. Haven't you heard?"

Furious, William pushed his seat away from the table on the church's lawn and stood.

"William?" Katherine asked. "Where are you going?"

"To tell my mother to sit down. It's time to eat."

He stormed off. Awkwardly, everyone at the table looked at each other. Some bowed their heads.

"He isn't even here, and he's causing problems," Katherine's mother said.

"Mother?"

"If he pulls his juvenile pranks tomorrow, I'll have his delinquent ass thrown out! William warned me about him!"

"Mother! Sssshh!"

"Excuse me," Ray said, looking uncomfortable and easing away from the table, before disappearing inside the church.

At the church entrance, Sandra stared out the open door. William slowly approached and draped his right arm over his mother's shoulder. She didn't look at him. She continued to gaze out to the quiet roadway that led to the church.

"Come to dinner, ma," he politely said. "The food's ready."

"I'm worried about Jonathan," she replied, still not looking at him.

"Let's eat. The others are waiting."

"I'll be there in a minute."

"You know, he may not show up."

Ray appeared. He glanced at William who shrugged and shook his head.

"Sandra, come back to the table."

She turned and stared at them but didn't say a word. William and his father looked at each other. Sandra turned away and again stared outside. With discouraged looks, William and his father returned to the dinner table.

After a few minutes, a taxicab appeared. Jonathan got out, smoking a cigarette. He wore a stained sports coat and the same pink shirt from the night before.

His face was beat up; his hair was half-cut. He was filthy. As he approached the church, his mother intercepted him.

"Jonathan?" she said in a disappointed tone.

She opened his jacket and read the shirt, before taking his hand. His fingers were covered with ink from fingerprinting. She gently tried to straighten out his tousled mop of hair.

"Your clothes? Your hair? What happened to the $300 I gave you?" she asked. He said nothing. "Where's my car?"

"Is there a can in this place?"

Before she could answer, he disappeared into the church. She dropped her head.

Jonathan stood at the sink in the ornate men's restroom and shaved with the pink razor. The bathroom was immaculate. The fixtures were gold-plated. The floor and wall tiles were marble. Katherine's father briskly entered the room. As Jonathan shaved, he gazed from the mirror at her father who pissed at a urinal. They coolly stared at each other like two boxers before a championship fight. Katherine's father finished pissing and joined Jonathan at the sink area.

"You can relax, buddy," Jonathan spoke up as Katherine's father washed his hands. "I'm not the one marrying your daughter."

"Thank God for that," he said, shaking his hands dry and staring at himself in the mirror.

"She'll never know what fun she's missing," Jonathan mumbled out of the side of his mouth. "William can be a real bore if you know what I mean.

13

But I'm the real deal. The jackpot. The brand-new sports car behind door number one."

"Yeah, I bet you are."

Jonathan had joined the rest of the group at the table in the yard behind the church. Most everyone had already eaten. He stuffed a napkin in front of the "*Princess*" T-shirt and devoured the food on his plate like a steam shovel, washing it down with large gulps of the expensive red wine. Everyone else around the table remained quiet, trying not to stare. He looked like a man who hadn't eaten in days. Glancing up from his plate, he pointed to a piece of steak on a plate.

"Anyone goin' to eat that?"

Nobody said anything as he stabbed the meat with his fork.

"Slow down, Jonathan," whispered Sandra. "There's plenty to eat."

"I got to get it in me when I can," he said with a mouthful of food.

"Jesus!" William moaned, appearing embarrassed.

He glanced at his mother and rolled his eyes. She looked away. Jonathan paused from eating and looked over to William.

"You'll wake up tomorrow with the option for breakfast. I may not," he said, before searching the dinner table and pointing to a bottle of ketchup. "Can someone pass me that over here?"

Looking disgusted, Katherine's mother shook her head. Ray grabbed the ketchup bottle and handed it to him. Jonathan dumped large globs of ketchup over the steak. Everyone watched. Sensing everyone was staring at him, Jonathan glanced up and gazed around the table before nodding and holding up his glass of wine.

"Here's to Billy and his bride-to-be, Kimberly."

"Katherine," Sandra corrected him.

"Katherine," he mumbled with a mouth full of food and his wine glass held high.

Reluctantly, everyone lifted their glasses except for Katherine's mother. Her face was red with rage.

"I didn't think ol' Billy would ever do it," Jonathan teased.

"Jonathan?" Sandra whispered from the side of her mouth, worried about what he might say.

Everyone around the table looked uncomfortable. William glared at Jonathan.

"To find the time to get married, what with all the snotty noses and sore throats running around the city, the early morning hospital rounds, the afternoon tee times, the young nurses and their big tits."

Katherine's mother coughed on the wine she was drinking, nearly spitting it out of her mouth. William dropped his fork. Jonathan looked at Katherine and smiled.

"But I can see why. Holy hell, girl. You sure are one fine looking lady."

Katherine's mother slammed her hand on the table.

"Jonathan!" Sandra shouted.

Jonathan stared at Katherine. He winked as he took a big drink of wine. She politely smiled, looking somewhat amused.

"I knew my brother was successful, but I never thought he could hook himself a bombshell like Katherine. Damn."

Grinning, Katherine shook her head but didn't speak. Jonathan continued to stare at her.

"You're a knockout, Katie," he said in a more serious tone. "You're beautiful. You are. And I bet sweet. I can tell. I need a little sweetness in my world."

They stared a moment before Jonathan looked at William.

"So, what's a man do the night before he ties the knot?" he asked as William glared at him. "If you're interested, I know a girl who can really polish a knob, if you catch what I mean."

"Jesus Christ," William responded.

With both fists clenched, he pushed away from the table and stood. Jonathan dropped his fork and rose from his seat.

"That's enough, Jonathan," Sandra hollered. "Stop it!"

William stared at Jonathan a moment before stomping away.

"I need to piss," Jonathan grumbled, angrily tossing his napkin on the table, before walking away, fuming.

"If that monster comes to the wedding," Katherine's mother warned. "I'm staying home."

"Mother," Katherine exclaimed.

Jonathan stepped out of the bathroom, zipping up his pants. William waited for him. Before Jonathan could blink an eye, William was in his face.

"You'll never forgive me, will you? We were young."

"I blame the girl as much as you, but my own fucking brother," Jonathan interrupted. "I looked up to you, Billy. You were my hero."

"I said I was sorry."

"Sorry will never be enough. You just don't get it."

"I only invited you to the wedding because of mom."

"Do you think I even want to come?"

"Don't fucking come then."

"Oh, I'm coming."

"Then you better show up on time. And you better be sober. It's the biggest day of my life."

"Biggest day of your life?" Jonathan laughed. "Is that what you're telling everyone? What a load of shit."

William forcefully shoved Jonathan in the chest. Jonathan started to retaliate but stopped. They stared a moment. Without warning, William slapped Jonathan. Jonathan lowered his head and held his hand over his mouth. Looking up, he wiped at a trickle of blood that dripped from his nose.

"After tomorrow, don't you *ever* come around me again."

Jonathan watched as William walked away from him and stormed out of the church into the backyard. He then looked down at his stained hands before studying the stupid shirt he wore. He walked to the back of the church and peered out the door as the guests gathered their belongings and prepared to leave.

He stepped outside. Cars were lined up in a parking lot at the side of the church. The guests were led to their cars by church attendants. Jonathan watched as his mother and father were helped into a van that carried many of the family members of the wedding party. Neither looked back. He wished that they would have, not to offer a ride, but maybe just to wave, something, anything, to acknowledge his presence. But he got what he deserved. Their lack of acknowledgement was his own fault, and he knew it. He was the one who blew their $300, lost his mother's car, got arrested, and made a spectacle of himself at dinner.

William stood by the other cars and shouted out directions. The vehicles slowly began to drive away. William finally got into a car in the back of the line. Inside the car, Katherine turned and scanned the area, noticing Jonathan who stood alone by a church doorway.

"Should we invite your brother to the party?"

William glanced in the rearview mirror but didn't respond as he slowly pulled the car away. Alone, Jonathan watched as the cars disappeared from the lot.

Jonathan finished mopping the floors of a dark and musty boxing gym not far from his tiny apartment in the Tenderloin. He emptied a filthy muck bucket of water into an iron-stained sink and wrung out a frayed, gray mop with his hands. He wiped his hands on the front of his pants and walked to a back room. Charlie, a frail, elderly black man, sat on the bed.

"Johnny, Johnny, what's you doin'?" Charlie asked in a disappointed tone. "What's you go and get arrested again for? Thought you'd growed up by now. Shit."

Jonathan stared at the floor unable to look Charlie in the eyes.

"Are you as disappointed as I am? Huh? Are you? Look at me, boy."

Jonathan reluctantly glanced up.

"You gettin' in trouble tonight? Huh?"

"Not tonight, Charlie."

Charlie eased himself back in bed.

"Can you stay a little longer? I ain't been feelin' that well. Jus' stay with me 'til I fall asleep."

"I'm right here."

"Don't disappoint me again, Johnny. You hear me?"

Jonathan nodded as he helped Charlie ease back into the bed, covering him with a thick blanket and quilt.

William and Katherine stood in an open doorway of a lavish hotel suite. They pulled away after a long, passionate kiss.

"Next time we kiss," William said, grinning, "it'll be as husband and wife."

"I can't wait."

"See you at the altar."

Katherine nodded and backed into the room.

"What are you doing with the rest of the night?" He asked.

"Thinking about tomorrow. How about you?"

"Something quiet. I want to be well-rested for our big day."

They gazed at each other and smiled before she slowly closed the door. He stood at the door a moment before scurrying away. He glanced down the hallway in each direction before tapping on a door of another hotel room. The door opened to the smoky, cigar-haze of a loud poker game. Hundreds of dollars, bottles of whiskey, and cans of light beer covered the poker table. A cheer rang out as William entered.

"It's about time, lover boy. Now, take your seat."

William grinned broadly, rubbed his hands together, and sat down at the poker table.

"Tommy, call the girls. Billy's here."

The dark club was crowded and loud. Jonathan stopped there on his way home after working at the boxing gym. The rock band, Dirt Bombs, played their song, *"Chains of Love"*, on a stage in the back. Staring at a shot glass full of whiskey in front of him, he sat alone and smoked a cigarette at the bar. Several empty shot glasses were lined up next to a full draught of stout beer. He puffed hard on the cigarette, before stubbing it out. He glanced around the club, then knocked back the whiskey before draining the beer in one chug. The bartender approached. Jonathan shook his head and threw a $20 bill on the bar before leaving.

The morning streets were bright with the new day's sun. Businesses were just opening. Store owners hosed off the sidewalks in front of their establishments. Disheveled, Jonathan scurried by the many homeless men and women, lining the streets, looking for handouts. He checked his watch and sipped at a coffee. Reaching the boxing gym, he pulled on the door. It was locked. He pounded on the door.

"Charlie, Charlie," He pressed his face against the glass door. "Charlie. What are you doing? Let me in. Open up."

Hunched over, Charlie gingerly placed folded towels and assorted workout equipment around the gym's boxing ring.

"You're late," Charlie hollered. "Come back tomorrow."

"Charlie. Let me help you. Come on. Open up."

"Go away."

"Charlie, Charlie," Jonathan yelled, banging on the door. "Come on, Charlie."

Chapter Three
You Seem Like a Girl Who Needs More Than That

The heavy oak door of the historic brownstone church slowly opened. Jonathan eased himself into the foyer. He wore a wrinkled tuxedo shirt and slacks. The wedding ceremony was nearly over. At the gift table, he snatched a bow off one of the packages and stuck it on an unopened pack of cigarettes he pulled from his pocket. He scribbled out a note and stuck it on the cigarette pack. He then placed the cigarette pack on the table with other gifts.

Jonathan noticed a coat rack and checked out the hanging sport jackets. He pulled one from a hanger and slipped it on. Hearing a cheer, Jonathan opened the stained-glass door that separated a large foyer from the church. William and Katherine kissed before turning to face the wedding guests in the crowded church.

"Ladies and gentlemen," the priest proclaimed, "I introduce to you, the new, Dr. and Mrs. William Hayes."

The wedding guests stood and applauded. Jonathan lit a cigarette and disappeared out the front of the church by himself.

The wedding guests arrived and entered a beautifully decorated ballroom of a hip, art deco-style hotel near Union Square in downtown San Francisco. Jonathan stood with his mother by a table that was covered with the names of all the guests on small placards.

"Jonathan, get our card so we can sit down."

"Table assignment for the Hayes family?" he asked the young attendant.

"I have two cards," the attendant responded, studying the assignments. "One is for Ray and Sandra Hayes. The other is for Jonathan."

Jonathan took the cards.

"Where are we sitting?" Sandra asked.

"You and dad are at table 2. I'm at table 27."

"There must be a mistake," she said, taking the cards.

"There's no mistake, ma. You know that."

Jonathan sat at a table with strangers in the back of the ballroom near the entrance to the kitchen. Food servers hustled in and out of the busy, swinging kitchen doors. At the front, toasts were being given for the wedding couple.

"Now, who did you say you were?" a wedding guest sitting next to Jonathan asked.

"I'm the brother of the groom."

Everyone at the table stared at him. He suddenly pushed away from the table and stood.

"Excuse me. I have a toast to give."

Jonathan confidently strode towards the stage at the front. Katherine's mother spotted him. She sat up in her seat and leaned forward as he reached the stage, grabbing the microphone. Katherine's mother nudged her husband and pointed to Jonathan.

"Don't let him say a word."

Jonathan pulled out a stack of index cards and cleared his throat in the microphone that briefly and loudly squealed with feedback. The place went silent.

"I would like to say something for the other side of the family," he spoke into the microphone. "My name is Jonathan. I'm the brother of the groom."

William sat up straight and glanced around, appearing worried about what Jonathan might say. Next to him, Katherine's mother sharply elbowed his ribs.

"Do something," she said to William. "Stop him."

William shrugged, continuing to glance around, looking confused.

"When I was young," Jonathan went on, "I tried to keep up with my big brother. He probably doesn't know this, but he was everything to me," he spoke, checking his notes. "I wanted to be just like him. I was his shadow."

Katherine smiled and looked at William who sat expressionless.

"But as we got older, I fell behind. I couldn't keep pace with Billy. He went one direction, mostly up, a successful doctor, and I, well, went the opposite, just look at me."

The crowd chuckled as Katherine's father left his seat and approached the microphone. Jonathan noticed him but continued with the toast, talking faster.

"Now, upon finding his lovely new bride, Katherine, he has set the bar far too high for me. He has married the perfect woman."

Katherine's father moved next to him, reaching for the microphone.

"That'll be enough, boy."

"I'll never be so lucky," Jonathan went on, turning away from Katherine's father and ignoring him.

"Now, gimme that!"

Katherine's father grabbed for the microphone. Jonathan tried to fight him off.

"I don't really know Katherine that well, but …" Jonathan continued into the microphone.

"Now, gimme that!"

The two struggled for control of the microphone.

"But I'm not done yet," Jonathan grumbled.

They continued to fight for the microphone. Others approached. Katherine called out. Chaos quickly ensued.

"Dad. Stop. Please," Katherine called out. "Let him finish." She turned to William. "Do something. That's your brother."

William stood but didn't leave his spot at the table.

"Now, give it," Katherine's father moaned, violently yanking at the microphone.

Trying to keep the microphone, Jonathan accidentally bumped into Katherine's father who awkwardly stumbled to the floor. William finally rushed to his father-in-law's aid. Jonathan checked the microphone.

"Give me the microphone and get the hell out of here," William shouted at his brother.

"Now, where was I?" Jonathan tried to continue.

William motioned for the bandleader to start into a song. The band began playing a loud version of the Stevie Wonder song, "*Signed, Sealed, Delivered I'm Yours*".

"I don't really know Katherine that well, but …," Jonathan continued into the microphone, but his words were drowned out by the music as William ripped the microphone from Jonathan's hands.

"I wasn't going to say anything bad."

Holding a glass of whiskey, Jonathan smoked a cigarette, sitting alone on a bench outside the hotel. In her wedding dress, Katherine appeared and pointed to the cigarette.

"Can I have one of those?"

He handed her a cigarette.

"You're going to love my wedding gift."

He lit the cigarette for her as she took a seat next to him.

"How's your wedding going?"

"It's been fun. Did you eat?" she asked as he shook his head. "Do you want me to get you something?"

"I'm not hungry."

"You gave a beautiful toast."

"I didn't get to finish it."

"I wanted to apologize but couldn't find you."

"Apologize?" he asked, studying her with a puzzled look.

"For my father, my mother …"

"I meant everything I said in the toast," he interrupted.

"Let me hear the rest of it."

He took a long drag on the cigarette.

"Come on," she prodded.

"I can't," he said, shaking his head.

"Why not?"

"I'm embarrassed."

"Embarrassed? You don't seem the type."

He shook his head.

"Come on."

Reluctantly, he pulled out the index cards.

"From the beginning?"

"Where you left off."

Jonathan looked at the notes and hesitated before beginning.

"I don't know Katherine that well …"

He stopped and glanced up at her. She stared back.

"You have the brightest brown eyes I have ever seen."

"Go on with the toast," she said after a brief pause, not taking her eyes from his.

He looked to the notes.

"But I have learned a great deal about her in the short time that I've been around her," he said, pausing a moment. "I get a lot of stares and funny looks from people who don't know me, mostly because I don't dress like them, I don't talk like them, and I don't live like them."

He paused again and looked up from the notes. A smile creased her lips as she stared back at him.

"Don't look at me like that," he said.

"Like what?"

"The last young woman who looked at me that way ruined my life."

"Finish the toast."

He looked back at the notes.

"But Katherine doesn't see me like most people do. Maybe she's a little naïve, but she looks at me with interest, curiosity, and respect. It's a look of acceptance. I know that look."

He stopped and shook his head.

"I can't go on."

"Please."

"I can't."

"Come on."

He gazed at the notes a moment before starting again.

"Because I live the way I do, I've become a pretty good judge of character. And Billy has hit the jackpot. Katherine is warm, gentle, caring, intelligent, good-hearted ..."

"You don't even know me," she interrupted.

He glanced up. They stared at each other for a moment before he looked back at the notes.

"God, my brother is lucky. I would give anything to be him today."

He raised up the drink he was holding.

"With all my love ..."

Katherine stared and smiled. Feeling awkward, Jonathan looked away and took a drink.

"Those are the nicest words ever written for me."

"I mean everything I said."

"I know you do."

She leaned over and gave him a hug. Jonathan awkwardly pulled away from her and stood.

"Shouldn't you get back in there?" he asked. "You're the star of the party. It's your night to shine."

"Can I have those notes?"

He shrugged and handed them to her.

"I'll put them in the wedding scrapbook," she said, studying the notes.

"What are these other lines on the bottom here?"

Jonathan glanced at the notes and grimaced.

"Oh, yeah. Those. Those were reminders …"

"Raise up drink," she interrupted, reading the list. "Chug it. Shake groom's hand. Hug bride. If she likes the toast, *hang on tight. Don't let go*?"

A puzzled look crossed her face.

"I got to take whatever I can get, man. A wedding can be lonely affair without a date."

She shook her head and smiled.

"You are an interesting character, Mr. Jonathan."

He shrugged, lighting a cigarette.

"Can I get another one of those?"

He handed her a cigarette and started to walk away.

"Where you going?"

"I need to go," he stopped and turned.

"Maybe we could grab a coffee sometime," she said, somewhat to his surprise.

"Sure."

There was an awkward silence for a moment before Jonathan spoke up.

"What is it about Billy?" he asked, studying her. "I know, he's handsome and successful, and …"

"He will always take care of me."

"You seem like a girl that needs more than that."

They stared as she took a long drag from the cigarette.

The frosted glass doors to the honeymoon suite of the swanky hotel burst open to the sound of laughter and giggles. William carried his new bride through the living room and directly into the bedroom. Beaming and still in her wedding dress, she carried an unopened bottle of champagne and two glasses. She kicked off her shoes as he threw her onto an oversized bed. He quickly crawled on top of her and began to nibble her neck and ears. She dropped the champagne bottle and reached for the lamp on the nightstand.

"Can we keep the lights on this time?" he asked as the bottle of champagne rolled across the floor away from the bed.

Still dressed in the clothes he wore to the wedding, Jonathan entered his dark, messy apartment alone. He opened a mostly empty refrigerator and grabbed three cans of Miller High Life that were connected by a plastic six-pack ring. He crawled through an open window onto a rusted, cast-iron fire escape that was four stories above ground.

Noise filled the night as the city bustled below. Car engines hummed. Taxicab horns annoyed. Sirens howled in the distance. He wished to silence the laughter and conversation from faceless strangers who strolled by, hidden in the blackness below him.

He cracked open the first can of High Life and took a pack of cigarettes from his pocket. Before digging out a cigarette, he counted them to see how many he had left. He finally shook out a cigarette and lit it, before taking a long and satisfying draw of smoke. He put the can of cold beer to his lips and nearly drained it in one gulp. He sighed, wishing he had more beer and another pack of cigarettes.

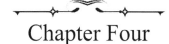

Chapter Four
Don't Be Afraid to Be Yourself

With tropical drinks, Katherine and William lounged in the white sand of a secluded Caribbean Island beach, staring into the crystal blue ocean water. The playful beat of the reggae classic, "*The Tide is High*", by the Paragons could be heard from a cabana in the distance. Katherine wore a skimpy black bikini and was very tan. William, too, was proud of his lean, fit body, sporting nothing but a pair of tight swim trunks. They were a striking couple.

"I would like to get to know your brother better," she said, not looking at her new husband.

"Who?" he asked, after taking a sip from his fruity cocktail.

"Jonathan."

"What for?"

"There's something about him."

"There's nothing there," he shook his head, "trust me."

Despite last call, the Tenderloin dive bar, The Tam, was especially busy. Bar patrons circled the long wooden bar and clapped their hands. All eight beer taps had been turned in the opposite direction and opened. Beer poured from the taps onto the bar surface and flowed from one end of the bar to the other. Laughing with his arms stretched high into the air, Jonathan stood on a barstool at one end of the bar.

The bar regulars counted out in unison, "One! Two! Three!"

Jonathan dove headfirst onto the bar covered in flowing beer, sliding its complete length through the sudsy foam before crashing over the end into a stack of empty beer kegs and cardboard boxes. Everyone loudly cheered and laughed. With his right arm raised and fist pumping the air as if in victory, Jonathan stood and staggered out from the fallen kegs. He was covered in beer, dripping wet. The bar crowd cheered louder.

It was early morning and still dark outside. Jonathan slept on the floor in the middle of the mess of his apartment. It had been weeks since the place had been swept and dusted. It had been even longer since the trash had been collected and taken out. Unlocked, the front door to the place quietly opened.

Charlie hobbled in, leaning heavily on his cane. He kneeled close to Jonathan's face and pulled out a whistle. Emptying the air from his weak and aged lungs, he blew the whistle with all the strength he could muster. Jonathan shot up like a missile into a sitting position, trying like hell to figure out where he was and what was going on.

"Get up, boy," Charlie barked. "You got one hour 'til your court date! Get you ass up!"

Wiping his eyes, Jonathan fell back onto the floor and groaned.

"It's time you pay the man, Johnny. I'm not lettin' you miss this one. No sir."

In a dated and small, paneled courtroom, Jonathan stood in front of a bloated, gray, and humorless judge. Unshaven with a black eye and shaggy hair, Jonathan wore the sport coat he had stolen at the wedding. Charlie sat in the back of the room.

"The charges that have been filed against you include solicitation of a prostitute, indecent exposure, possession of a controlled substance, and causing a public nuisance," the judge unenthusiastically read from a sheet of paper.

He paused and looked up at Jonathan who glanced behind him. Charlie shook his head in disappointment.

"How do you plead to the charges?"

"No contest, your honor," Jonathan mumbled in defeat, looking back to the judge.

The front desk at the county jail was busy. The front door opened, and a somber-looking Jonathan was escorted through by a deputy sheriff. The correctional officer at the front desk quickly recognized him.

"Hey, fellows," the cop called, grinning, "look who it is."

In no mood for jokes, Jonathan shook his head and tried to avoid eye contact with a group of deputy sheriffs and city policemen crowded around him. The deputy handed one of the desk cops some paperwork as Jonathan emptied his pockets.

"How's Snooki?" the cop joked.

Katherine sunbathed alone poolside. Her skin, covered in suntan oil, glistened in the baking sun.

Carrying golf clubs, William appeared from the outside cocktail bar accompanied by a pasty, white-haired stranger. With a puzzled look, Katherine lifted her sunglasses.

"You don't mind getting lunch without me, do you?" he asked. "I found a partner."

"How long will you be gone?" she asked, squinting into the sunlight at William's new friend.

"I'll be back in time for dinner."

She didn't reply, only half grinned. He smiled.

"Thanks, honey. I knew you'd understand."

She slightly nodded without expression and watched him walk away. She glanced around the deserted pool area and played with the straw in her drink.

With his head in his hands, Jonathan sat in a damp, moldy jail cell. A guard approached, carrying a tray with meat stew, a ham sandwich, green beans, and a carton of milk. Jonathan didn't acknowledge the cop until he rapped on the bars of the jail cell. Jonathan scanned the cop and the food, before returning his head to his hands.

"Chow time, Hayes! The best part of your crummy day."

"I don't want it," he said, not lifting his head to look at the cop.

"You got to eat," the guard replied as he started to slide the tray of food through the open horizontal slot in the bars of the cell.

"I said I don't want it," Jonathan snapped, looking up and staring at the guard.

"But the taxpayers want you to have three square meals."

"I'm not goin' to eat it, so don't waste it. Give it to some other chump in here."

"I wouldn't starve myself over bangin' a whore."

"Who's starvin' themselves? I'm only here for 72 hours. I've gone longer than that without food."

"Whatever," the guard said, moving to the next cell. "Hey, McIntyre, you want another plate of food?"

The greasy hulk of an inmate who had knocked Jonathan out a few days before eagerly moved to the front of the cell. The guard slid the plate of food to him.

"It seems Hayes is too good for jail food."

Jonathan slammed his foot on the pedal of the toilet causing it to flush. He did it again.

"I would stop if I were you," the guard warned. "Remember what happened the last time you played this game?"

The two stared a moment. As the guard turned to leave, Jonathan stomped on the toilet's pedal one last time. The guard stopped, stood still for a moment, before finally walking away without turning.

Back in her own king-sized bed after the weeklong honeymoon, Katherine rolled over and reached for William. He wasn't there. Puzzled, she sat up and glanced around the room, searching for him. It was still dark outside. She glanced to the clock.

"What time is it?" she whispered to herself, rubbing her eyes.

Quietly navigating the large, dark house, she crept downstairs and heard a noise. She also sniffed a few times. She smelled something. Smoke. Glancing around, she heard the noise again and noticed a slip of light from underneath the door that led to the garage. As she walked toward the light, the smoky smell became stronger. She stopped at the door before slowly pulling it open. Puffing a cigar, William cleaned a set of golf clubs.

"William?"

"What are you doing up so early, hon'?" he asked with the cigar dangling from his mouth.

"Couldn't you do that later?" she asked, shielding her eyes from the bright fluorescent lights of the garage.

"I don't have to be at the clinic for a few more days. I'd like to see the guys. Between the clinic and the wedding, you know, I haven't …"

"Today?" she interrupted.

"I have an early tee time."

"When will you be home?"

They stared a moment until his attention returned to the golf clubs. Slowly closing the door to the garage, she knew what the answer would be. He didn't have to say it, but she made sure to ask.

Appearing out of place, Katherine entered a grungy apartment building in the Tenderloin. She stepped over a sleeping homeless man who snored in the lobby. White duck feathers strangely were stuck to the greasy handrail of the stairs. The place reeked of rotting vegetables, body odor, and all the detergents and air fresheners used to try to hide it. The elevator was broken. As couples argued and babies wailed, Katherine hiked up four flights of stairs and found the door to Jonathan's apartment. She knocked. There was no answer. She knocked again. Still, there was no answer. She turned. Suddenly, Jonathan appeared in the hallway behind her. He looked pale and gaunt. The beard on his unshaven face had thickened. He seemed exhausted.

"What are you doing here?" he asked, intently studying her.

"Do you want to get a coffee?"

"Where's Billy?" he asked, glancing around.

"I'm alone."

"This isn't the best time," he paused. "I just got out of jail."

They stared. He expected her to leave at that point, but she didn't.

"Come on, let me get you a coffee. It looks like you need one."

"Didn't you hear me? I just got out of jail," he went on as she shrugged. "Who sent you here?"

"No one."

Jonathan slid by her and unlocked the door to his apartment.

"It wasn't for anything violent," he said, before entering.

"Huh?"

"Jail. I didn't do anything violent."

An awkward silence followed as they studied each other.

"Are you sure about the coffee?"

"I just need to be alone right now."

"Here's my number," she said, scribbling on a small slip of paper and handing it to him. "Another time?"

"Sure."

They again stared a moment. She finally walked away but glanced back a couple times to check on him. As he entered his apartment, he wadded up the piece of paper she had given him and tossed it on the floor.

It was a brisk but beautiful weekday morning. There wasn't a cloud in the bright blue sky. William and three buddies golfed the busy and challenging course at the local country club not far from his palatial home in Marin County across the bay from San Francisco. The foursome looked sharp in khaki dress slacks and light cotton sweaters. They each wore a different color. As the others waited on the green of the 2nd hole, William chipped his ball, nearly buried in deep sand, out of a bunker 20 yards from the hole and watched it roll within inches of the pin. He raised his right arm in triumph with his sand wedge high over his head as if he'd just clinched the U.S. Open. His playing partners cheered.

"Now, that's how it's done," he boasted.

"It's good to have you back, Billy Boy."

"It's good to be back."

"You might actually be dangerous if you could get out here more often."

"You'll see me more. Don't worry about that. I'm cutting back on my hours at the clinic."

"You deserve it."

"Damn right, I do."

At a free health clinic, a sickly Charlie sat with welfare mothers and their crying babies in a crowded waiting room. Jonathan stood at the front desk, trying to answer questions asked by a busty young nurse.

"Why is Mr. Robinson here to see the doctor?" the nurse quizzed him.

"He's got a chest cold- cough, congestion, trouble breathing, you know, everything like that."

"Your relationship to the patient?"

Jonathan turned, glanced at Charlie, and thought for a moment, before saying, "brother?"

Looking very ill, Charlie shook his head and shrugged, not looking amused. Also, not amused, the nurse glanced up from the form she filled out and asked again.

"What is your relationship to the patient, Mr. Hayes?"

She stared at Jonathan.

"Pain in my ass," Charlie called out.

"I'll just put down, 'friend'," the nurse said, not looking up from the form. "You can take Mr. Robinson back to see the doctor now."

Jonathan helped Charlie up from his seat. As they started to go back to the examination room, the nurse called out, "Mr. Hayes, I need your signature."

"After we're all done here," Jonathan flirted as he signed the form, "you wouldn't want to go grab a bite to eat or get a drink, would you?"

She ignored him, taking the form, rolling her eyes, and walking away.

"I guess a blow job's out of the question, then?"

"Johnny," Charlie snapped, slapping him across the back of the head with a hard right hand. "Grow up, boy. Jesus. Don't you never learn nothin'?"

William and his playing partners were standing next to the tee box at the 7th hole, waiting for a slow-moving threesome in front of them to finish the hole. A bright orange golf cart, wrapped in an advertisement for a popular brand of citrus vodka, suddenly approached with an attractive young lady named Jessica behind the wheel.

"Thirsty, boys?" she called out, bringing the cart to a stop.

"Four lights, please," William said.

Jessica hopped out of the cart. She was in her early 20's and had long blonde hair. She wore a revealing golf outfit with a tight low-cut top and a very short skirt that didn't leave much to the imagination. At the back of the cart, she purposely bent over and reached into a cooler of ice and pulled out four bottles of beer as William and his buddies leered.

"That'll be $24, Dr. Hayes," she said, reaching the beers to him.

"Put it on my membership tab," he said, passing out the beers to the group.

"I'll stop back in a few holes," she said.

"We hope so," William said, grinning.

As she returned behind the wheel of the golf cart, William hurriedly followed before she could drive off and secretly handed her $40 for a tip.

"You working later?" he asked quietly, glancing back to the others.

"Yeah, three o'clock."

"Dining room or bar?"

"I'll be outside at the golf course bar 'til eight, Dr. Hayes."

"I'll see you there."

She glanced to the other golfers before nodding to William with a smile and a wink.

"And stop calling me, Dr. Hayes," he said before she could drive away. "Makes me sound old. It's Bill."

In the back room of the gym, Charlie shivered in bed with the covers pulled up to his chin. Several prescription bottles littered a small nightstand beside him. Jonathan filled a humidifier with water before plugging it in. Steam instantly bubbled from the gurgling water bath. Jonathan took a seat in a chair next to the bed and stared at Charlie, who had his eyes closed. Jonathan didn't know if he was asleep or not.

"Johnny?" Charlie called out, opening his eyes and scanning the room.

"I'm right here, buddy,"

"You're like a son to me," he said, before shaking his head. "What you goin' to do when I'm gone?"

"You're not going anywhere, Charlie."

"I worry about you. I don't wants to worry about you no more."

"I know. I know."

"You need to change," he said as Jonathan looked away. "You're the only one that can do that."

Jonathan stayed until Charlie's eyes slowly closed. He clicked off a light and grabbed the mop and water bucket that leaned against the wall outside the room.

With little enthusiasm, he swished the mop across the floor of the gym, occasionally dipping it into the bucket's filthy water. He stopped mopping at a pay phone near the entrance of the gym. He pulled from his pocket a crumpled slip of paper. With a dripping, dirty mop in one hand, he dialed the phone with the other, glancing at the number on a piece of paper.

At an upscale coffee shop in Ghirardelli Square near Fisherman's Wharf, Katherine and Jonathan sat at a table, sipping coffee. Katherine looked great. She was tan, fit, and immaculately dressed. Jonathan, on the other hand, looked like a disaster. His eye was bruised and scarred; his dirty hair was still unevenly cut. He hadn't shaved in weeks. He was pale. It appeared as if he had lost a significant amount of weight since her wedding day. He wore the pink "*Princess*" T-shirt and the sports coat he had taken from the church. Both were weathered and filthy.

"I've wondered," she asked, studying him, "what do you do?"

"What do I do? What do you do?"

"Me and my life and the way I live it are rather obvious, I would think. I know nothing about you. How do you get money to live?"

"I work a few hours every day in a boxing gym."

"Is that enough to live on?"

"And …," he shrugged, but paused.

"And?"

"Everyone has needs. In my world, everyone's a little more desperate. I just provide them with what they need."

"Drugs?"

"Maybe, a little weed here and there," he said with a shrug, "but there's so many other things."

"Do you steal those things?"

He took a sip of coffee before answering.

"You writing a book? Who's been asking?"

"No one. I'm just curious."

"I have ways of acquiring certain items and services for needy individuals," he said. "Sometimes for a price, sometimes for a favor. I try to help my peers."

"So, what are these items?"

"Anything from cars to women to money to cigarettes. Whatever."

"Cigarettes?" she grinned. "Thanks, by the way, for the wedding gift. I smoked the whole pack while we were away."

"You and Billy must have been getting busy."

"We had our fun."

"I bet you did," he teased.

"Stop it," she laughed. "It was great to finally have some time alone with William. He's always so busy with the …"

"Don't tell me shit like that," Jonathan interrupted. "Jesus, if I was Billy, I would never leave your side. Ever. I could stare at those pretty brown eyes of yours all day and never get bored."

She smiled and looked away, seeming embarrassed by his remark.

"Out of the hundreds of gifts we received," she said, looking back, "yours will be the only one I'll remember. Who gives cigarettes as a wedding gift? And your toast, it was unforgettable."

"I didn't get to finish it."

"Everyone has needs, huh? What do you need, Jonathan?"

He uncomfortably glanced away.

"I don't know, a shower, a haircut," he answered, "they'd be a good start, I suppose."

"Come on, what do you *really* need?"

He looked back and stared before answering.

"Nothing. I don't need anything."

"Come on, you said it," she pressed, "everyone has needs."

He still didn't respond.

"Why won't you tell me? What are you afraid of?"

"I'm not afraid of anything," he confidently replied.

"Why do you live the way you do?"

"Why do you live the way you do? Who's to say that my way of life isn't the right way?"

"It isn't normal."

"I don't want to be like everyone else," he shot back. "My brother's a doctor. There must be fifty thousand doctors in San Francisco. Who cares? There's plenty just like him. You meet him, he's forgotten. You meet me, well, nobody forgets me."

"Nobody forgets the freaks in a freak show either," she said. "Maybe you're a little jealous."

"Jealous? Hah …," he chuckled before his voice trailed off.

There was a short silence as they each took a sip of coffee.

"William's a damn good doctor. His patients love him. He's a good man. I'm lucky to be with him."

"I'm sure he tells you that all the time. Maybe I am a little jealous. Billy had it easy. I've had to struggle. And lately, the struggle has worn me out."

"He's had to work really hard and really long hours to get where he is. And he still works hard and long hours. You had choices."

"Maybe. But you must admit, he doesn't appreciate what he has."

An awkward silence followed as they stared.

"Does Billy even know you're here?" he asked, but she didn't respond. "Why didn't you tell him you were coming to see me? I don't think Billy appreciates you."

"Of course, he does," she snapped back.

"What do you do all day when he's at the clinic?"

"I have my friends, and I have …"

"It must get boring in your big house all alone every day," he interrupted. "Let me take you out sometime."

Katherine gazed at him with a puzzled look.

"No, no, no," he shook his head, "not as a date, as brother- and sister-in-law. Nothing against Billy, but you're missing out on some good times. There's a great big world out there."

"William and I go out. We travel."

"Not to my world. Come on. One time."

"I can't," she shook her head.

"You should."

"I just can't."

"Come on. Don't be afraid to be yourself."

"What do you mean by that?"

"Do you know what the most common deathbed regret is?" he asked as she shrugged. "It's- 'I wish I had the courage to live a life true to myself and not the life others expected of me'."

"That isn't me."

"Bullshit, it is. Come on."

"I really can't."

"Come on," he pressed her. "Meet me out. One time."

She slightly grinned but continued to shake her head.

"You have the worst poker face."

A smile creased her face.

"Let me think about it."

"No fun has ever come when someone has 'to think about it'."

She smiled and nodded.

"So, when's a good day for you?"

"How about Friday?" she answered without hesitation.

"This Friday?" he asked, appearing surprised she agreed. "The day after tomorrow, Friday?"

"Yes, this Friday."

"Now, I'm not talking about an hour or two."

"I'm free all day on Friday."

"Are you going to tell Billy?"

They stared at each other for a moment before she answered.

"Of course."

Staring at her phone, Katherine sat alone at the coffee shop. Her coffee cup was empty. Jonathan was gone. She reached for the phone and dialed it.

"Hey, babe," she spoke into the phone. "What are you doing for dinner tonight? I thought I would meet you downtown- someplace nice. I'm missing you. We haven't gone out since we've been back from the honeymoon."

Holding his phone to his ear, William turned away from the outdoor bar not far from the country club's 18th hole. Jessica, the young server, stood behind the bar, waiting on a handful of bald or graying and mostly out of shape middle-aged men. A half-eaten burger and fries sat on a plate in front of William.

"Jeez, hon'," he answered in a quiet voice, stepping away from the bar as Jessica watched. "You better get something without me tonight. I'm catching up on some patients' notes and treatment plans."

"But you're off today. I thought you went golfing. You don't have to be back to the clinic until next week."

"Yeah, I know, but …" he said as his voice drifted off for a moment. "After the morning round, I was feeling guilty. You know I'm so far behind."

Katherine didn't respond. A brief silence followed.

"I'll be home in a few hours," he went on. "I'll see you then."

She still didn't respond, turning off her phone.

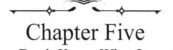

Chapter Five
You Don't Know What Love is

Jonathan studied a profile picture of his brother from a news release. In the photo, William wore a designer tie and a pristine, perfectly pressed white lab coat. He smiled proudly. As always, he appeared clean, neat, and important. Jonathan studied his reflection in the grease-stained oven door window in his kitchen. He didn't have a mirror in his apartment. He noted his ragged appearance, touching his shaggy hair and unshaven chin. Unlike his brother, he looked damaged, tired, and uneven. At the refrigerator, he opened the freezer door, reached in, and pulled out a plastic Ziploc bag. The bag was filled with $20 bills.

With a new, tight haircut, Jonathan stood among racks of shirts at an upscale downtown men's clothing store. He flipped through the shirts and picked one he liked. He held the shirt up against his chest and studied it. In the middle of the store, he shrugged and pulled off the shirt he was wearing. A store employee approached.

"Can I help you?"

"Nah," Jonathan shook his head, standing there topless.

"There's dressing rooms in back."

"I'm good here."

Jonathan pulled on the new shirt, walked to a mirror, and checked himself out. He shook his head and took off the new shirt. Again topless, he flipped through the other shirts on the rack. The store employee rolled his eyes and walked away as other customers stared at Jonathan.

The sun had just come up. With a loud rev of the engine, Jonathan pulled into a parking spot in front of the boxing gym, riding a silver and black, vintage 1974 BMW R 90 S motorcycle. Charlie stood in the doorway and watched. Jonathan shut off the bike and entered the gym.

"Where'd you get that thing?"

"Some dude owed me a favor. When I tried to return the bike, he was gone. No one knows where he went."

"You goin' go and kill you'self. That's what you'll do."

"I won't be in to work later," Jonathan said, "but you're all set for today."

"I seen that," Charlie replied, studying Jonathan and his fresh appearance. "Why you so cleaned up?"

"I got some business to take care of."

"Good or bad?"

"Hopefully, good."

They stared a moment.

"Are you sure you don't need me today? I know you've been sick."

"I'm good. I'm good."

Before Jonathan could walk away, Charlie called out.

"I worry about you, Johnny."

Jonathan stopped and turned.

"You don't need to worry anymore."

Fidgeting, Jonathan paced the front porch of the mammoth and immaculate house where William and Katherine lived. He wore a black leather jacket, new buttoned-down shirt, pressed jeans, and black motorcycle boots. The house was in the hills of an exclusive neighborhood across the Golden Gate Bridge from the city. He could see the San Francisco Bay in the distance from the porch.

After a few nervous minutes, he finally knocked. The door opened, and Katherine appeared. As always, she looked stunning. She wore a brown suede jacket, tight-fitting jeans, and cowboy boots.

"Whoa," she exclaimed, seeming surprised by Jonathan's fresh appearance.

"I can look pretty good sometimes," he said as they awkwardly gawked at each other for a moment. "We still on?"

Katherine nodded, stepping out of the house and pulling the door shut behind her. She abruptly stopped upon seeing the motorcycle parked in the driveway.

"Maybe, I should drive."

"Come on."

"I don't know," she shook her head as she studied the bike.

Jonathan reached a helmet to her.

"I'll be careful."

Reluctantly, she took the helmet. Jonathan got on the bike and kicked started it with a loud roar of the engine. She shook her head again and shrugged.

"Come on."

After pausing for a moment, she looked around before putting the helmet on and climbing onto the bike behind Jonathan. Appearing uncomfortable, she searched for a place to put her hands, eventually resting them on her thighs.

"You may want to hold on," Jonathan said, looking back. "This isn't a toy."

He motioned to his waist before revving the engine. She grabbed hold of him as he wheeled the bike around the driveway and drove off.

The heavy fog had burned away with the morning sun. The motorcycle zoomed over the mostly empty and rolling highway of the Marin County headlands that was lined with tall walnut and redwood trees. A trace of the city skyline as well as the orange-painted steel from the top of the Golden Gate Bridge appeared in the distance. Jonathan grinned as the speeding motorcycle sliced the cool morning air. He checked back to Katherine. She smiled. He gunned the bike causing her body to slightly jerk backward. She clutched his waist more tightly. He laughed as she slapped at his shoulder.

Soon the blue, choppy waters of the San Francisco Bay appeared before them, shining under the sunlight of the bright new day. Reaching the Golden Gate Bridge, Jonathan pulled the bike off at an exit in Sausalito to a popular spot where tourists gather to take pictures of the bridge before crossing into the city. He drove them further up a hillside to Battery Spencer where both the bridge and downtown skyline could be viewed. Jonathan parked the motorcycle, shut down the engine, and hopped off. Katherine tried to follow.

"Wait, wait," he told her. "Stay there. Now, give me your phone."

Appearing puzzled, she shrugged but pulled the phone from the pocket of her jacket and handed it to him.

"Now move up on the bike," he directed her, "like you're driving it."

She scooted to the front of the bike and reached for the handlebars. Under a brilliant blue sky, the distinctive, one-mile-long bridge was framed behind her. The sun beamed brightly. She looked as if she were sitting in the middle of a colorful picture postcard. Everything was nearly perfect.

"Now, smile," he said as she half-grinned. "Come on. Like you mean it."

Her grin blossomed into a smile then a laugh as he snapped several pictures. He checked the digital photographs and nodded with approval before walking the phone back to her. As Jonathan joined Katherine at the bike, an elderly man who had been taking photos with his wife approached.

"Can you take our picture?" the man asked, holding out his camera and motioning to his wife.

Jonathan nodded and took the camera. The man wrapped his arm over his wife's shoulder. With the Golden Gate Bridge prominent in the background, the couple smiled as Jonathan snapped the picture.

"Thank you, sir," he said, taking back the camera. "It's our 50th wedding anniversary today."

"You guys are adorable," Katherine said.

"How long have you two been together?" the lady asked Katherine.

Before answering, Jonathan and Katherine glanced at each other.

"Thirty minutes," Jonathan said.

On a blanket among one of the blooming public gardens of the Golden Gate Park, Jonathan and Katherine sat together. They had spent a good portion of the morning, hiking for several miles through a flower conservatory and different gardens, including the famous San Francisco Botanical Garden. The park was quite active. Numerous folks walked dogs or pushed babies in carriages. Couples held hands and carried gourmet coffees as they casually strolled the many paths of the winding, wooded park. Laughing and yelling, kids chased each other. Earthy twenty-somethings tossed Frisbees or played guitars. Jonathan even recognized a few of the homeless gentlemen who appeared to be living in the lesser traveled areas of the park.

The ends of two strings were anchored in the ground in front of Jonathan and Katherine as kites flew high overhead.

"It's been a long time since I flew one of these," he said.

"I love this park," she said. "I love this area. It's so vibrant, so romantic."

"I've always liked it, because no one bothered me here."

"Have you ever been in love?" she asked as he gazed to the kites above.

Jonathan laughed and held out his arms, "Who would love me?"

"Come on, have you ever been in love?"

"Just a few weeks ago," he said. "It was a long weekend."

"Seriously."

"I am serious. I met this woman on a Friday. I was in love 'til Tuesday."

"That's not love."

"A lot can happen in four days."

"Did she feel the same?"

"Until her boyfriend caught us," he nodded. "I still think about her. She could suck a tennis ball through a straw ..."

"That's not love," Katherine interrupted. "Come on. You must've been in love at some point."

"When did you and Billy meet?" he changed the subject.

"My first year in college."

"What'd you major in?"

"Education."

"So, you're a teacher?"

"I'm certified but haven't actually teached in a classroom."

"Why not?"

"William doesn't think I need to work."

"What?"

"He makes good money, and he feels I should stay home."

"Yeah, but it's not his life."

"I know, but ..."

"Would you like to teach?" Jonathan interrupted.

"I think so. Maybe not forever, but I love kids."

"If you want to teach, then you should teach."

"It's not so simple. William wants me available whenever he has some free time. He works so hard."

"What was your first reaction when you saw him?"

"What?"

"What was your first reaction when you saw Billy?"

She didn't respond at first, tilting her head and thinking for a moment.

"Come on. You're thinking too hard. This guy would be your husband."

"That was so long ago."

"You don't forget the first time you see or meet the significant people in your life."

"What was your first impression of me?"

"I couldn't stop looking at you," he said without hesitation, his eyes locked on hers. "I knew I had to look away. But I couldn't. And when you did catch me staring, your reaction let me know it was all right to keep looking." He paused as they continued to study each other. "What'd you think of me?"

"I didn't expect you to look like you did, but," she said, "your personality lit up the church when you walked in. You were the life of the rehearsal dinner. Maybe not in a good way, but certainly life of the dinner."

"You were the only one there bright enough to get the joke."

"So, your life and the way you live are nothing but a joke?"

"I never intended it to be that way. But the joke is getting stale," he again changed the subject. "Have you always lived in the bay area?"

"I've lived all over the world. Wherever my father's business took us. I never made any close friends growing up as my father didn't stay in one place for too long. We moved to San Francisco at the time I started college."

"Was there anyone before Billy?"

"What?"

"Was there anyone before Billy?" he asked, making a gesture by pushing his right index finger in and out of his curled left fist. "You know?"

She didn't immediately respond.

"Oh, no."

"Well …," she said with a shrug as her face turned red. "Not really."

"No."

"What?"

"How old were you?"

"Huh?"

"The first time," he pressed. "How old were you?"

"Jonathan?"

"Come on, how old were you?"

There was a long pause before she answered.

"Why is it so easy for me to tell you these things?" she asked. "I've never told anyone any of this."

"How old?"

"20."

"20?"

"The first time I had sex," she nodded. "I was 20 years old but going on 16. I was so inexperienced. I didn't know what I was doing."

"Billy, right?" he asked as she nodded. "Did you enjoy it?"

"Of course," she instantly answered.

"Bullshit. When was the first time you really enjoyed it?" He teased, but she didn't respond. "I know what you need."

"Stop it."

They stared a moment.

"And I now know what you need," she countered.

"Tell me, what do I need?"

They stared at each other until Jonathan glanced up at the kites, bobbing in the wind.

"I'll tell you when you're ready."

Katherine followed Jonathan into the lively boxing gym not far from where he lived. Several boxers worked out, skipping rope, punching speed bags, or doing push-ups. Every three minutes a bell would ring, and the boxers would move to different training stations. In the ring, Charlie taught a young boxer some moves. He shuffled his feet, bobbed his head, and threw phantom right- and left-hand punches at the air.

"Charlie? What are you doing?" Jonathan called out. "The doctor told you to stay off your feet until you felt better."

"When I goes to work," Charlies responded, wiping sweat from his forehead, "I *goes* to work."

"You feeling better?"

"Nope."

"Then get out of there and come sit down."

Charlie gingerly slid through the ropes as Jonathan helped him out of the ring.

"I didn't think you was comin' in today?"

"I brought someone here to meet you," he said, motioning to Katherine. "This is Katie, Billy's wife."

"It's actually Katherine," she said, correcting Jonathan.

Grinning, Charlie took her hand.

"Lordy, lordy, lordy. Mm-mm-mm," Charlie grinned, then pointed at Jonathan. "What's you doin' with this crazy fool?"

"This is Charlie."

Charlie kissed her hand before backing away and checking out her whole body. He held out his arms.

"Gimme a lil' sugar, honey."

Katherine smiled as they embraced. Charlie tightly held onto her.

"Uh-huh," he yelled out, looked to Jonathan. "You can go away now, boy. Everything is jus' fine. I ain't never lettin' go, Johnny. I ain't never lettin' go."

Leading Katherine, Jonathan entered the Tam, his favorite Tenderloin dive bar, like a king. A rousing hello greeted them. As the jukebox blared, he nodded and smiled as they walked through the dark, smoky bar. The bartender approached them. She had short blonde hair. A series of tattoos covered both of her arms. She grinned upon seeing Jonathan.

"Hey, Johnny."

She leaned over the bar and kissed him on the cheek. Katherine glared at the bartender, appearing somewhat jealous.

"Looking good," the bartender remarked, studying Jonathan's neat appearance. "Tequila?"

Jonathan looked at Katherine who nodded. The bartender poured two generous shots.

Katherine intently watched the bartender.

"These are on me," the bartender said with a wink.

Jonathan took one of the shots and slid the other to Katherine. They lifted the shot glasses.

"Here's to brothers, sisters, and tequila."

They gulped down the shots and grimaced. Katherine shook her head. Jonathan pulled out a pack of cigarettes.

"Mind if I smoke?"

"Only if you don't offer me one."

He handed her a cigarette and lit it. The bartender returned with the tequila bottle and filled the two shot glasses.

"Who's your friend, Johnny?" she asked, looking at Katherine.

"This is Katie. She's married to my brother."

"It's actually Katherine," she said, reaching her hand out to the bartender.

"Where's your brother?" the bartender asked Jonathan as she shook Katherine's hand.

"Protecting the city from sickness and disease."

"I didn't know you had family."

"Yeah, can you believe it?" he nodded. "Katie's the only one with balls enough to hang out with me."

Jonathan grabbed the shot glass and held it up. Katherine did the same.

"Thanks for making me feel like part of the family."

"Here's to a fun afternoon," she added.

They touched glasses and downed the tequila. Both grimaced.

"Shots of tequila never get easier," he groaned.

They each puffed on their cigarettes. Jonathan spun around on the stool and faced away from the bar.

"You know, a stupid kite changed my life," he quietly confessed, not looking at Katherine.

"How so?" she asked, intently studying him.

"One day during my last year of high school," he said, still not looking at her, "I skipped all my classes to fly kites with a young lady I had just met." He looked at Katherine. "So, yeah," he said. "I've been in love before."

"I don't think it was the kite that changed your life."

"She broke my heart."

"How'd you meet?"

"I went to a freshman orientation at a college in the city. I had accepted a scholarship to play baseball there. She was one of the tour guides for the orientation and …," he paused.

"And?"

"I didn't finish high school. I lost the scholarship and never went to college."

"You didn't graduate from high school?"

"And I was number one in my class."

"How long did the relationship last?"

"We lived together for a year."

"How did it end?"

"She started screwing someone else. Tried to hide it from me."

"Did you know the guy?"

"Didn't know him," he said, shaking his head.

"What'd you do?"

"I lost it. I wandered through the city in a daze. I had plenty of time on my hands. Plenty of time for no good. It's been that way ever since. Nearly eight years and counting."

They stared at one another for a moment.

"Thank God for the boxing gym and Charlie."

"Charlie's so cute."

"He's a saint, man. He's bailed me out of jail. He's collected me from the bars and shooed away the bad guys."

Neither said a word for a moment.

"All because of some stupid girl."

"She must've been some girl."

"I thought so."

"Love can be mighty powerful."

"A mighty powerful sword," he said. "Look at me now. What a mess."

They stared as the bartender approached.

"One last shot."

"This has to be my last."

The bartender filled their shot glasses. They knocked back the tequila. Katherine coughed, and Jonathan laughed.

"Why are you here with me?"

"You need to spend more time with William and your family."

"You didn't tell him that we were meeting, did you?"

She shook her head, scanning the crowded bar. He lit another cigarette for her.

"If you sit here long enough," he said, "you'll see the whole city walk in."

"How did you find this place?"

"I needed a home."

"Do you see your family much?"

"Not really."

"Why don't you go home?"

"I can't."

"How come?"

"Who's been asking?"

"No one," she said, shaking her head. "I'm curious."

"Are you hungry?" he asked, abruptly changing the subject.

"Starving."

"I got some cash on me. Let me take you some place nice."

"I'm bored with nice places. Take me some place different."

As the sun slowly disappeared over the rolling hills in the distance across the bay, Katherine and Jonathan walked along the creaky, uneven planks of a wooden pier that extended over the water. They followed a long string of round and brightly illuminated clear bulbs that hung from the side pilings of the pier to an amusement park. The central attraction of the park was a three-story high Ferris wheel that flashed from red to blue to white then gold as it deliberately spun to the screams of the kids at the top of it. Katherine ate a hot dog as they strolled among the bright, flashing lights of the rides and carnival games. The music of the Buddy Holly song, "*Everyday*", competed with the distinct summer sound of a steamboat calliope playing in the distance.

"Your parents never took you to a carnival?"

Katherine shook her head. She had mustard on her lip. Jonathan motioned for her to stop. He gently wiped it clean with a napkin.

"God, I feel sorry for you," he said. "When we were old enough, my parents would drop me and Billy off here on summer mornings. We'd blow the whole day. When they'd come to pick us up, we'd hide on the rides. They could never find us."

Laughing, Katherine tossed plastic rings, trying to win cheap prizes attached to wooden pegs. The rings bounced everywhere. After she threw all the rings, she looked to Jonathan. He would hand the game attendant more money for another set of rings.

"We'd spend our summers in Paris or Barcelona," she said, flipping the rings.

"That sounds rough," he said sarcastically.

"But I lost all those years," she said, still tossing the rings but not circling any pegs. "I had no brothers or sisters."

She stopped tossing the rings and turned to Jonathan.

"Those were lonely times. I never got to be a kid. I had nobody my own age to hang out with."

She focused back on the game and tossed the rings again.

"There's nothing worse than being in a fabulous place and having no one to enjoy it with."

"I think the same thing every morning," he said. "This city can be a lonely place when you're always by yourself."

"Can I ask you something?"

"Sure."

"Why did you introduce me as Katie at the gym and the bar?"

"I don't know," he said with a shrug. "Katherine sounds so formal. Katie seems more fun."

"My grandmother called me, Katie? She hated the name, Katherine. I think she had a crazy aunt Katherine or something like that."

"Yeah?"

"Yeah. My happiest times spent as a child were with my grandmother," she said, still tossing the rings. "She gave me the attention that was missing from my parents. She died when I was young."

"How old were you?"

"I was nine. Still, the saddest day of my life. It took me a few years to get over it. She was such a kind and generous soul but also strong and independent. She spent most of her life volunteering to help others. Even raised a few foster kids. There was not a hateful bone in her body. I wish I could be half the woman she was. I look at my life. I've done nothing."

"Does Billy know this?" he asked as she shook her head. "You've never talked about your grandmother?"

"He wouldn't care," she said, tossing the last ring in her hand.

"Come on. I think Billy's an asshole and all, but he's not that bad, is he?"

The last ring she tossed suddenly landed over one a wooden peg.

"Hey. Look at that. I got one."

The game attendant retrieved the prize from the peg and handed it to her. It was a cable car keychain.

"A memento of this day," she said with a smile, before handing it to Jonathan.

It was late. Night had fallen. The concession stands were being boarded up. Many of the rides had shut down for the evening and were no longer operating. The amusement park was about to close. Katherine and Jonathan sat upon different colored horses of a brightly lit, slowly moving carousel. He studied her until she turned towards him.

"What are you thinking about?"

"You know, this is the closest I've ever come to riding a real horse," he confessed. "We're not that different."

"How so?"

"We're both full of regret," he said. "I regret all the stupid shit I ever did. I'm a spent Roman Candle who long flamed out."

"And me?"

"You regret all the things you haven't done. You're like the flower that never got to fully bloom."

"That's not exactly true."

"It is."

"I did miss out on my wild years," she said. "I never figured out who I was. The most rebellious thing I ever did was sneak off to buy cigarettes after my parents went to bed. I wish I was fifteen again."

"Then don't waste the rest of your life."

"I don't really know you, but you're probably the most self-aware person I've ever met."

"Hah. I'm a disaster."

"I don't see you that way."

"I drink too much. I smoke too much. I'm rude. I screw marginal women. I'm unemployable. And now, I'm exhausted."

"It's not really you," she said as the ride stopped. "You know that."

"I need to get you home."

"I'm not ready to go home yet."

With a confident, purposeful pace, William strolled the back corridors of the country club that were usually reserved only to the club's staff. He looked as if he were on a mission in search of something or someone. At a door with a sign that read, 'Employees Only', he glanced over each shoulder in both directions of a hallway before entering without a knock. Easing the door open, he walked into what appeared to a break room of some sort with a coffee pot, water cooler, refreshments, and an assortment of plush couches and chairs. Jessica was the only one in the room. William approached from behind her as she prepared a coffee. She abruptly turned as he neared.

"Dr. Hayes? Didn't you read the sign? Employees only."

"Like I said, call me, Bill," he replied, standing awkwardly close to her.

"What are you doing in here?" she asked, not backing away. "It's late. Shouldn't you be at home?"

"I was searching for you."

"Yeah?"

"Yeah."

"For business or …?"

"You could say business," he interrupted.

"What do you need?"

"I need a bartender."

"Why me?"

"Come on," he said, extending his arms out to her. "You're the best."

"What's the gig?"

"The club poker tournament."

"Not interested," she said, shaking her head.

"Come on," he pleaded.

"I've done it before. It wasn't worth it."

"What do you mean, not worth it?"

"They paid me my hourly wage plus tips. But most everyone lost all their money at the poker table. It wasn't a good night for tips, and I stayed there almost until daybreak as everyone spent the night trying to win their money back," she said, shaking her head. "Nah, I don't think so."

"What will it take for me to get you there?"

"I'll do it for $300 and tips."

"I'll see what I can do," he said, smiling. "I'll see if Lenny will take the $300 out of the player buy-ins. Shouldn't be a problem. It wouldn't be the same without you."

"I appreciate it, Dr. Hayes."

"Please call me, Bill."

"Thank you, Bill."

Grinning, he continued to stand awkwardly close to her almost as if in a daze.

"Bill?" she said as he stared at her.

"Yeah?"

"You probably should leave now. Only the employees are supposed to be back here."

"Right, right," he nodded as she backed away from him.

Inside a liquor store in the Mission District, Katherine paid for an expensive bottle of cabernet. Her wallet was open. It contained hundreds of dollars. Jonathan waited outside. He sat on the motorcycle and revved the engine to keep the bike from stalling. Katherine dashed out of the shop with the wine and hopped on the back of the bike.

"Where are we headed?" she shouted over the noise of the bike's rumbling engine.

"Up there," he pointed. "In the hills above the fog."

With Katherine on the back, Jonathan wheeled the motorcycle around into a clearing on the edge of a wooded hill that overlooked the fog-covered city. They sat on the bike and gazed at the magnificent view before them. Jonathan glanced at Katherine. She grinned, studying the beautiful San Francisco night. He then nudged her with his elbow and pointed to a grassy meadow behind them. The area was filled with flickering lightning bugs. Katherine's smile grew as she watched.

"This is where fireflies come to fade away."

"How did you find this place?"

"Because of the fog at night and always being in the city, I rarely see the stars. I wanted to know what was up here behind the fog."

He paused as they gazed, mesmerized by the blinking lightning bugs.

"A misplaced colony of fireflies," he said, "as lost as any of us."

"It's beautiful, so peaceful."

"When I first discovered this place, I imagined the fog to be heaven, and the fireflies to be the stars."

She glanced over and studied him. He looked away.

"Now, where's that wine?" he asked.

As she handed him the bottle, she mumbled, "Shit."

"What?"

"No corkscrew."

"No problem," he said, taking the bottle.

He walked to a tree and began forcefully pounding the bottom of the bottle against the trunk.

"I learned this from a homeless guy who lived for years only on stolen wine," he said, glancing back at her. "He never ate. He was a goddamn miracle of science."

He again struck the bottle against the tree.

"Will this work?"

He smacked the bottom of the bottle against the tree again

"Trust me."

He hit the tree again with the bottle.

"Be careful! You're going to break it! That was expensive."

"How expensive?"

"$85."

"$85? Shit. That's about 80 more than I spend on the wine."

He banged the bottle against the tree harder.

"Jonathan! Be careful!"

He checked the cork. It had started to work its way out of the top.

"One more."

He struck the tree with the bottom of the bottle The cork was halfway out. He pulled on the cork until it came out with a pop.

"And you doubted me," he said, reaching the bottle to her. "You get the honor. Take the first hit."

"Right out of the bottle?"

"Yeah, right out of the bottle. Where do you think we are?"

She took the bottle and studied it, before sniffing the wine.

"We just can't swill it like this. We need to let it breathe a minute. All that pounding probably damaged it."

"Give me the damn bottle."

She handed it to him. He put it to his mouth and took several very large gulps.

"Not bad," he said, wiping his lips. "I think it survived just fine."

He handed her the bottle. She stared at the top of it with a funny look.

"Who are you trying to kid? Everyone drinks wine for the same reason."

"And that is what?"

"To get stupid. It's called self-medication. Now, drink up."

She slowly raised the bottle to her lips and took a drink.

"Come on, Katie. This ain't no country club social. Drink it. Like you mean it."

Grinning, she took a long chug of wine. After she lowered the bottle, wine dripped from her chin.

"That a girl."

Wiping her lips, she handed him the half-emptied bottle.

"Like I always say," he said, studying the body. "One bottle of wine is never enough."

The large suburban house was quiet. No lights were on. Nothing moved. Wearing a polo golf shirt and a pair of matching slacks, William unlocked the front door and went inside. Looking puzzled, he glanced around the dark, empty house.

"Katherine?" He called out, setting a handful of golf tees and a scorecard on the kitchen counter. "Katherine?"

Watching the fireflies, Jonathan and Katherine sat close together, leaning against a tree.

"I'm cold," she said, pulling her arms in close to her body.

Jonathan took off his leather motorcycle jacket and draped it over her shoulders. The lightning bugs continued to flicker around them. The empty wine bottle had rolled away, out of their reach. He handed her a cigarette.

"Last one."

He lit it for her. She took a long drag and handed it back to him. He took a puff.

"Have you ever been in love?" he asked.

She didn't respond, reaching for the cigarette and taking a long pull.

"Well, have you?"

"That's a silly question to ask me," she answered. "You know I love William."

"Really? You love what he is and not who he is. You love your lifestyle with him."

"That's not true."

"You love the fact that your friends and family think he's handsome and successful. You love that he's a doctor and makes good money."

She looked away from the cigarette and stared at him.

"You don't know what love is," he went on.

He reached for the cigarette and took a long drag before handing it back.

"Tell me then, what is love?" she asked.

"Love will make you do things you never thought you would do. Love will change who you are."

She looked away.

"You'll know when you're in love. It's a speeding train, roaring down the tracks out of control. No brakes. It's losing your breath, dropping out of the sky. Like falling from an airplane. No parachute."

She took the last puff of the cigarette before putting it out.

"Love is hit and run, and not knowing what hit you," he continued before pausing. "It's like being struck by lightning."

She looked back to him.

"I don't think you've ever been in love."

"I love your brother."

"How do you know? You started dating him when you were just a kid."

"So."

"You're not in love. I doubt you're even friends."

She glanced away and flicked the spent cigarette to the ground.

"You're more like his shadow," Jonathan pressed.

"I don't like where this conversation is going."

"You only do what he does."

"That's not true."

"The thing about a shadow is, it doesn't speak. It doesn't think."

Now agitated, she stood and began to gather her things.

"A shadow has no soul."

"Stop it!!"

"I know what you need."

"I need to see my husband. Take me home."

In the black of night darkened by tall pines that blocked out the moonlight and stars that smeared the sky, the motorcycle raced over the deserted highway across the bay from downtown with a roar. Katherine wore Jonathan's leather jacket. She held tightly onto his waist. Her long, dark hair danced with the wind from underneath the helmet, blowing away from her head. Jonathan focused straight ahead, not taking his eyes from the road.

Jonathan slowed the bike as they approached her house. Looking both bored and agitated, William sat in a recliner in the dark and repeatedly flipped through the channels of the television. He sat up upon hearing the motorcycle.

Jonathan stopped the bike and watched Katherine as she hastily slid off the back of the bike. Without acknowledging him, she started for the front door.

"Hey?" he called out.

She stopped and turned. He tossed her the cable car keychain. She caught it.

"I had the best time today."

She didn't respond. They studied each other for a few seconds. She slightly nodded before turning for the house. At a quickened pace, she rushed towards the door. Jonathan wheeled the bike around and pulled into the street. He revved the engine a few times and watched her disappear inside.

Wearing Jonathan's leather coat, Katherine pushed the front door open and entered. She briefly glanced at William who was blank-faced and silent, threw her keys and purse on a table by the door, and brushed by him without saying a word. She stomped up the stairs and entered a room with a slam of the door. William quickly turned and peered out the open front door. Across the street, Jonathan continued to rev the engine of the bike, before eventually peeling away.

"Asshole," William mumbled under his breath as he watched from the door.

Glancing over his shoulder, he reached for Katherine's purse on the table, opened it, and took out her phone. After typing in her security code, he opened the photo application. Again, he peeked over his shoulder before slowly thumbing through her library of recent pictures. He stopped and studied one of the photos of Katherine sitting atop the motorcycle with the Golden Gate Bridge behind her. She hadn't appeared that happy since their wedding night.

Chapter Six
This Is Not Over

William quietly entered the bedroom with a tray of dry toast and black coffee, waking Katherine who was buried in a tangle of blankets and sheets. Her tousled hair covered most of her face. She slowly opened her eyes but didn't turn to him. She was terribly hungover.

"Aren't you supposed to be at the clinic?" she mumbled into the pillow under her face with a dry, sour-tasting mouth.

Holding the tray, he sat beside her on the edge of the bed.

"You need to put something in your stomach."

"What are you still doing here?" she asked, still not turning to him.

"I got someone to cover for me."

He nudged her. Dehydrated and looking ill, she turned and faced him. He held out the tray.

"Eat something."

She shook her head.

"I didn't do anything against you yesterday."

"I'm going to cut back on my hours."

She turned and rolled away from him. He stared at her a moment before setting the tray on the nightstand and leaving the room.

Jonathan slept on a ragged couch in his apartment. As always, the place was a wreck. Pounding on the door woke him. He slowly dragged himself from the couch and staggered to the door. The pounding continued.

"Hold on. Jesus."

As he eased the door open, William barged in and grabbed Jonathan by the neck with both hands, forcing him against a wall. Jonathan struggled as his brother violently slammed him repeatedly against the kitchen counter.

"What in the fuck were you doing with my wife last night?"

"Get your hands off me," Jonathan yelled, struggling to free himself from his brother's tight grip.

"What were you doing with my wife?"

"I said get your hands off me. I'll fucking destroy you if you don't let go."

William released him, then forcefully shoved him against a kitchen table. Jonathan nearly fell over, before regaining his balance. He rubbed at his red and scratched neck.

"What in the hell were you doing with my wife last night?"

"Ask Katherine. It was her idea."

"I know what you're trying to do."

"Come on. Look at me, man," he pointed around his pitiful apartment. "Look at this place. What could Katherine possibly see in me? You got it all. You're holding all the good cards."

"Don't fuck up my life …," William paused as they stared each other down, both with their fists

76

clenched. "Stay away from me. Stay out of my life. And most importantly, stay away from my wife."

"Katherine," Jonathan interrupted.

"What?"

"Your wife's name is Katherine."

They continued to stare. William, his face red with rage, stepped closer. Their faces were inches apart. It was a standoff. Each waited for the other to make a move.

"Call her by her name when you speak of her."

William slightly grinned, then chuckled with a shake of his head, before turning to leave.

"You must be jealous," Jonathan spoke up. "For you to come all the way here to the bad side of town."

Without warning, William wheeled around and sucker punched Jonathan with a solid right hook to the jaw, knocking him to the floor.

"Shit," William yelled in pain, shaking his right hand repeatedly while clenching and unclenching it.

On the floor, Jonathan shook his head and blinked his eyes several times. Blood seeped from the corner of his mouth. He tried his best to stand, but he couldn't get his wobbly legs underneath him enough to lift himself off the floor.

As Jonathan tried to regain his senses, William glanced around before discreetly pulling a lady's wallet from his coat pocket. He noticed a cluttered bookcase and placed the wallet on a shelf. He quickly headed for the door as Jonathan called out, still on the floor.

"This isn't over."

William stopped before leaving but didn't turn.

"Oh, it's over," he hollered back, before violently slamming the door shut.

Katherine stood at the front of a long line at the supermarket with a shopping cart full of groceries. She frantically searched through her purse with a puzzled look as the cashier started to ring up the many items she intended to purchase. Frustrated, she shrugged and looked up to the unsympathetic cashier.

"I can't find my wallet."

The cashier annoyingly sighed, stopped scanning the food items, and glared at her. The folks in line behind Katherine audibly groaned.

"It should be here. I don't know where it could be."

She continued to go through the purse and then her jacket pockets.

"I won't be able to pay for these things without my wallet."

"Manager to aisle seven," the cashier called out over the intercom.

The people in line behind Katherine moaned louder and quickly dispersed, looking for another register.

With a bruised and swollen jaw, Jonathan mopped the floors of the boxing gym. Coughing and wiping sweat from his head, Charlie sat in a metal folding chair next to the ring and barked out instructions with a hoarse voice to young boxers. Charlie glanced to Jonathan.

"What happened to your face?"

"I got caught with my guard down."

"I thought I taught you better than that."

"My opponent fights dirty."

"I *know* I taught you better than that."

Fumbling with his keys and appearing exhausted, Jonathan walked down the hallway that led to his apartment. He was greeted by two plain-clothes police detectives at his door.

"Are you Jonathan Hayes?" one of the detectives asked, holding up his badge.

"What now?"

"We got a warrant to search the apartment."

"Come on in," Jonathan said, unlocking the door. "I got nothing to hide."

The two detectives followed Jonathan into the apartment and glanced around.

"The maid's been on strike," Jonathan joked.

The detectives immediately began opening and closing drawers, closets, and cabinet doors. They shuffled through yellowing newspapers, outdated magazines, and stacks of personal documents that were scattered about.

"What are you looking for?" Jonathan asked. "Maybe I can help."

"We're searching for a wallet and/or the contents of the wallet."

"Wallet? There's no wallet here. I never have enough money for a wallet."

One of the detectives retrieved a lady's wallet from the top shelf of a bookcase. He studied the wallet and opened it.

"Is this your wallet?"

The wallet was empty except for a driver's license and a few other identification cards.

"Huh?" Jonathan said, appearing puzzled. "I've never seen that wallet in my life." He noticed Katherine's picture on the ID card. "Katherine?"

"So, you know Ms. Hayes?"

"Well, yes, she's …," Jonathan started to say, before stopping himself.

Both detectives stared at him. He shrugged.

Handcuffed, Jonathan dejectedly sat on a bench in the crowded, noisy police station. He angrily jerked at the cuffs locked around his wrists that were positioned behind his back. He called out to the officer at the front desk.

"I can clear this up. Let me make one call. You owe me one call. I've been through this before. I need to get out of here."

The cop at the desk in front of Jonathan ignored him.

"One freakin' call, man. Come on. This is bullshit. I need to get out of here. I can't stay here tonight. Not tonight."

The cop finally looked up.

"You're here too much, Hayes. There's no rush to put you back out there," the cop said, motioning to the front door of the station. "I'm tired of dealin' with your fuckin' ass every week."

"Come on, man. I didn't take the wallet."

The cop rolled his eyes and continued to work on the documents in front of him.

Tall, thin candles burned brightly in the darkened dining room. Not looking at each other, William and Katherine silently picked at their dinner of steak and baked potatoes at opposite ends of a long dining room table. They occasionally traded brief and awkward glances as they sipped their wine. Finally, Katherine placed her fork and knife on her plate and stared at William until he looked up.

"I'm sorry," he confessed.

"I have to be as important to you as your career and your golf game."

"Yes."

"So, our lives together will be different from this point on?"

"I promise. I will cut back on my hours at the clinic, like I've already told you."

Katherine placed her cloth napkin on the table and reached for the open bottle of burgundy, filling her glass.

"What happened to your hand?" she asked, gazing at the bandage wrapped around his right knuckles.

"Golf course accident."

They studied each other a moment.

"I don't believe Jonathan took my wallet."

"Believe it," he assured her, barely looking up as he wolfed down his dinner.

"But why would he steal from me? I thought we were friends."

"He has no friends. And he steals from everyone."

Katherine glanced at her food on the plate that she hardly touched and pushed it away from her. William refilled his wine glass, took a long sip, and studied her for a moment.

"What'd you two do all day?"

"Huh?"

"What did you and Jonathan do all day?"

"He showed me where he lived," she shrugged, "where he hung out, where he worked. We just talked."

"What did he tell you?"

"About what?"

"Me? Anything?"

"We didn't talk about you much," she said as he continued to study her. "He mostly talked about himself."

"He's a con man. You know that, right? He makes a living hustling people. That's how he gets what he wants. That's how he's programmed to survive."

"I think you're wrong about him," she said, shaking her head. "I spent a whole day with him. He's not like that, not like that at all."

"I know him better than anyone," he said, taking a bite of steak. "What did he tell you? Some sad story about heartbreak and missed opportunities. We've all heard it before. All lies."

"He sounded sincere."

"There's nothing sincere about him," he said, talking with his mouth full while cutting another piece of meat.

"I can't believe that."

"Then explain to me," William said, looking up, "what happened to your wallet."

They stared a moment.

"Did you cancel your credit cards?"

"Yes."

Katherine studied him closely, not taking her eyes from his. William didn't look away. She finally stood, took her plate, and walked into the kitchen. He

82

reached for the napkin on his lap and angrily flipped it on the table, before finishing the wine.

After a 36-hour stay in the county jail, Jonathan frantically signed a form before hurrying out of the station. It was foggy and dark night. With urgency, he darted and weaved through the evening dinner crowds that clogged the sidewalks. Reaching the gym, he gasped for air. The front door was unlocked. That was unusual as the gym should have been closed for the evening. He entered and glanced around the empty gym.

"Charlie? Charlie?"

He rushed to Charlie's room in the back, still calling his name.

"Charlie?"

He found Charlie kneeling beside his bed. Jonathan caught his breath.

"I didn't know you prayed."

"I don't," he shook his head. "I'm stuck. I drop my readin' glasses. So, I go down here to get 'em. But I haven't been able to get back up."

"Jesus, Charlie."

Jonathan leaned down, reached under Charlie's arms, and pulled him up before gently placing his stiff body on the bed. He grabbed a bottle of water and helped him drink some of it.

"How long have you been down there?"

"I don't know. Two, maybe three hours. I lost track."

"Charlie, Charlie."

"You always helpin' me out, Johnny. I would've closed this place down years ago," he said. "I's too old and crippled up to keep it going. You helped me out."

"Anything for you, Charlie," Jonathan said, taking a seat next to the bed. "But you need to be more careful if I'm not around."

"Trainin' boxers is the only thing I ever knowed. Shit. I never married. I never had kids. I trained boxers. That's what I do. I lived my dream."

"You talk like you're going somewhere."

"Each morning's a bonus round, Johnny."

"You need me to stay with you?"

"If you don't got nowhere to go."

"I'll stay as long as you need me."

Before long, both were fast asleep, Charlie in the bed and Jonathan next to him in the chair. By the looks on their contented and relaxed faces, they peacefully slept like they'd never slept before. Jonathan was exhausted after another overnight stay in jail. Charlie was worn out from too many years on earth.

A large conference room within the country club had been converted into a poker parlor. Four large round tables were arranged in the middle of the room and seated six players each who were all full-time members of the club. The tables were covered with cocktails, pints of beer, small plates of snacks, dirty ashtrays, and tall stacks of poker chips. Despite a permanent 'No Smoking' sign posted on the wall, several of the players enjoyed fine cigars, filling the room with a dense cloud of a pungent but sweet-smelling white smoke.

The stakes and emotions in the room were running high. To participate, each player was required to purchase a minimum limit of $1,000 worth of poker chips. Some players, like William, purchased several thousands of dollars' worth of chips in a desperate attempt to recover money lost in the early rounds of the event. A make-shift bar was set up in the back of the room. Jessica kept busy making a variety of different cocktails, pouring beers, and taking orders that she delivered in between poker hands. There was a tip jar in front of her on the bar filled with mostly $20 and $100 bills.

During a break late into the night after many hours and scores of poker hands, Jessica approached William, placing her hands on his shoulders, and softly caressing the tense muscles of his neck. He glanced back to see who it was as she leaned forward and blew her warm breath into his ear.

"Thank you," she whispered.

"Thank you?" he asked as he stared back at her with a flushed face and wired from a six-hour binge of gambling and alcohol.

"For the job," she said, pointing to the tip jar on the bar that overflowed with cash. "I owe you one."

He nodded as she briefly massaged his neck and shoulders.

"Do you need anything?"

Enjoying the massage, he nodded and held up his empty highball glass.

"And keep them coming," he said, handing her two $20 bills he pulled from his shirt pocket. "I'm not leaving until I win my money back."

"That could be years," cracked one of the players next to him at the table, grinning and sitting behind the largest pile of chips in the room.

Morning arrived gently without car horns, alarms, or the typical outside noises that were common in the neighborhood where the boxing gym was located. Jonathan opened his eyes. It took a few seconds to figure out where he was and how he got there. After clearing his head, he looked at Charlie. In a fetal position, Charlie's body was balled up and seemed dwarfed by the blankets and pillows around him. Jonathan instantly sensed something was wrong. He vaulted from the chair and scooped Charlie into his arms.

"Charlie. Charlie. Charlie!"

Charlie's limp, lifeless body didn't respond as Jonathan tried to shake his friend and mentor from slumber.

"Charlie! No! No! Oh, God!"

A young boxer suddenly walked into the room.

"Call 911!" Jonathan screamed.

The kid stared at him for a moment.

"Call 911! Goddammit!"

The kid rushed out as Jonathan immediately started to perform chest compressions.

"Come on, Charlie. Breathe, dammit. Breathe."

For more than five minutes, Jonathan continued the compressions. Holding Charlie's nose, he would blow into his lungs after every ten compressions. He didn't stop until the sound of a siren from an approaching ambulance wailed outside the building. He pulled Charlie into his arms and tightly embraced him.

Several paramedics rushed into the room, carrying emergency medical kits.

"Sir?" one of the paramedics called out. "Sir, can we check the patient?"

"I'm sorry, Charlie," Jonathan sobbed. "I'm sorry, so sorry. Charlie, please. Please don't leave me."

"Sir."

Jonathan gently released Charlie's body to one of the paramedics who checked for any vital signs of life. The other paramedic loaded a syringe and prepared a set of cardiac defibrillator paddles. After many seconds, the first paramedic motioned to his partner that nothing else would be needed. Jonathan dropped his head.

"I'm sorry, sir. He's gone."

Chapter Seven
I Can Sell Anything

It was the middle of the night. William had just finished a full day at the clinic and had another scheduled at 6:00 A.M. for the following day. He currently was on call and was exhausted. He slept soundly, but Katherine couldn't. She clicked on the light beside the bed. William awoke squinting and rubbing his eyes as he looked at her.

"You, all right?" he asked.

Without warning, she peeled the covers off him. He wore nothing but a T-shirt and a pair of boxer shorts. His initial reaction was to cover himself with his arms as if cold. Without hesitation, Katherine crawled on top of him, sat on his lap, and abruptly pulled the shirt over his head.

"Whoa," William muttered unexpectedly.

She lifted her flimsy nightgown off and tossed it over her shoulder.

"What's this?"

Excited, he entered her as she slowly started to rock her writhing body with his. He tried to sit up, but she wouldn't allow it, forcefully pushing him back onto the bed. She ground on him, at first slow, then faster, then harder. Panting, he tried to catch his breath. He reached up and wrapped his arms around her back, pulling her tightly against his chest. The phone in the bedroom suddenly rang. He tried to roll her perspiring body underneath his. She didn't allow that either, remaining on top and riding him until his entire body cramped in spasm, before going limp. Spent, he nudged her off as their arms and legs were tangled together. He looked over. Her sweaty body glistened in the light.

"Jesus, where'd that come from?"

On his back, he glanced up to the ceiling, breathing heavily. She studied the phone as it continued to ring on the nightstand beside them. After a few more rings, she finally reached it. But he stopped her, pulling her body back and firmly holding her. The phone continued to ring.

"Let me go."

"The voicemail will get it."

"Let me go," she repeated as he refused to ease his hold on her. "I said, let go."

With a frustrated look, he released her. She sat up and quickly grabbed the phone.

"Hello? Hello?"

No one was on the line. She hung up the phone and glanced at William. He had turned away. She clicked off the light and stared at the phone. He soon was asleep, snoring beside her. As he soundly slept, she tossed and turned most of the night and didn't fall sleep until sometime in the morning after he left for the clinic.

Chain-smoking cheap cigarettes, Jonathan paced at the entrance of the popular coffee shop near the wharf that Katherine frequented. The coffee he held shook in his hands. He looked like a wreck- his clothes were wrinkled, his hair unkempt. He hadn't slept. His eyes were swollen and red. His jaw was still bruised. He reeked of alcohol. He was desperate. He had been desperate before but never like that.

Katherine finally appeared as he knew she would. She was accompanied by two friends. They giggled and cackled as they approached. Surprised to see Jonathan, Katherine immediately stopped before entering. With puzzled gazes, her friends stared at Jonathan, then looked at Katherine.

"Katherine?" one of her friends spoke up. "Are you good?"

"I'll join you guys in a minute," she answered, staring at Jonathan.

Her friends paused a moment before entering the coffee shop. Jonathan and Katherine continued to stare at each other.

"What's wrong with your jaw?"

"I didn't take your wallet."

"It was in your apartment."

"I wouldn't do that to you. I came all the way over here to tell you that in person."

"You lied to me in the park."

"Lied? About what?"

"You tell me."

"Who said I lied? Billy? Everything I said to you was true."

"That's not what your mother said. I was over her house. She said you finished school."

"But I didn't," he said, looking puzzled.

"Why would she lie?" Katherine pressed him, before pausing. "What else did you lie about? My wallet?"

He didn't respond.

"Goodbye, Jonathan."

She turned and reached for the door to the coffee shop. Before she could go inside, he grabbed her arm. She immediately yanked it away.

"Don't touch me. Don't ever do that again," she snapped as he stepped away from her. "And quit calling me in the middle of the night."

She again reached for the door of the coffee shop.

"It was a big mistake meeting you last Friday," she said, not facing him.

She opened the door, but before she entered, Jonathan said, "Charlie died yesterday."

She hesitated a moment without turning to him.

"I don't want to ever see you again," she said.

Before he could respond, she disappeared inside.

A closed gold casket was positioned in the middle of the ring in the boxing gym. The casket was covered with assorted floral arrangements and cards recently signed by many of the boxers who had trained with Charlie. Holding hands, several boxers stood around the casket and prayed. Jonathan watched from the back of the gym. He couldn't get any closer, wiping at the tears that filled his eyes. The guys in the ring started to sing an old Wanda Roth gospel song, *"God Pick Me Up."*

Just like a ship that's lost at sea
I need you Lord, where can you be
I just can't seem to find my way
Help Lord for I am weak today

God pick me up and let me stand

Please plant my feet on solid land
Alone I'm weak, with you I'm strong
Please hold my hand Lord and lead me home

Help me to know the wrong from right
Please light my way by day and night
That I may be a shining star
Just like the wise men from afar

God pick me up and let me stand
Please plant my feet on solid land
Alone I'm weak, with you I'm strong
Please hold my hand Lord and lead me home

As the song ended, Jonathan openly wept. He slid on a pair of sunglasses and quietly exited through a side door, leaving the gym for what he thought would be the last time. He had no idea what he would do next.

The Tam was dark and empty. Jonathan sat alone at a table in the back. The cracking, and sometimes skipping, sound of sad Tom Waits tunes blasted from failing speakers of a compromised jukebox. The Waits' CDs were worn from overplay, perhaps due to a longing of the bar regulars to be someplace else, anywhere other than the Tam. The place was unusually quiet for lunchtime. Jonathan's favorite bartender poured him a shot of tequila at the bar and walked it back to him, along with the bottle. She tried not to stare at his red, puffy eyes.

"Sorry to hear about Charlie."

"He was my last lifeline," Jonathan said, throwing back the shot.

"What are you going to do?"

"Something stupid I'm sure," he said, motioning for her to refill the shot glass. "Until then, it's jukebox and tequila."

It was a beautiful Saturday afternoon. Surprisingly, Katherine had persuaded William to cancel his golf outing for the afternoon. Instead, he agreed to take her to lunch. Not far from their home, they approached a small neighborhood pub, McSorley's Grill. Katherine had been curious about the place for years. It didn't matter the time of day. The parking lot was always full.

"Have you ever been there?" she asked while they were stopped at a red light.

"Where?"

"There," she pointed. "McSorley's. I've always wanted to go."

William glanced at the pub but didn't comment.

"Let's try it," she said as the light turned green.

He pulled the car through the intersection, and without slowing, drove past McSorley's.

"Hey. Stop."

"I thought we were going to the country club."

"We always go there."

"What about our member discount?"

"Hardly a discount with the prices they charge for a meal," she said, sounding exasperated. "You'd think you're 60 years old with your love of that place. It's like a funeral parlor there at lunch. I want to go somewhere that has a little energy. A place with some soul."

"And our loyalty points. We almost have enough points to get a discount on our membership fee for next year."

"Jesus, William, turn around."

"What?"

"Turn around."

"You serious?"

"We're going to McSorley's for lunch. So, turn around."

At the front door of his apartment, Jonathan pulled a note that had been taped to the doorknob. It read:

"You're out by the end of the week if no rent! It's been three months!"

He unlocked the door and entered. The place was a mess as usual. He walked into the kitchen, opened the freezer, and pulled out a plastic baggie of money. It contained a few one-dollar bills and a handful of quarters. Angrily, he threw the baggie back into the freezer and slammed it shut. Not having eaten much in days, he opened the refrigerator. There was nothing but a mostly empty Styrofoam container of Chinese takeout, an outdated jug of milk, and a couple pieces of rotten fruit. He rested his head against the refrigerator and stared at the pathetic contents. It was good he wasn't hungry. Since Charlie's death, he hadn't felt like eating.

He closed the refrigerator door and stared at the mess of his apartment. Grabbing a garbage bag, he began tossing away anything that he didn't want or wouldn't need. He knew he had to make a change. In no time, he had filled five large bags full of trash and set them out in the hallway of the apartment building.

Without hesitation, he also threw out several partially filled liquor bottles. There was no need to have any alcohol around, he thought. He already spent too much time in the bars.

After cleaning the kitchen and living room, he walked into the bedroom with a purpose. He opened the closet door and sifted through the hanging clothes. He grabbed a striped, green shirt, the sport coat he had taken from the church, a checkered tie, and a pair of brown slacks from the sparse closet. None of the items really matched, but he didn't have many other options, and they were all relatively clean which seemed to be the most important thing at the time. He spread the clothes out on the bed and studied them for a moment. He was ready for a new start.

Katherine excitedly entered McSorley's. William followed. The pub was dark but festive and very busy. The place had a loyal following of regulars from the nearby neighborhood. It was obvious several folks were there for baseball. Half of the televisions were tuned to the Giants game, and the other half broadcasted the Athletics game. But most people went to McSorley's for hearty portions of the many comfort food choices they offered.

The familiar aroma of frying bar snacks and grilling burgers filled the air. Grinning, Katherine led William to an open spot at the bar. The bartender approached.

"What'll be?"

"A tequila," she quickly answered.

"Tequila?" William questioned her with a puzzled look.

"A shot or in a drink?" the bartender asked.

"Shot."

"Any type? Reposado? Blanco? Or brand?" he asked as Katherine blankly stared at him, confused by his questions. "Or our well?"

"The well, that'll be fine," she said with an excited nod, before glancing back at William. "Tequila?"

"Whatever light draft you have," he said, looking to the bartender.

"Do you have any ones on you?" Katherine asked William as the bartender turned to fill the orders.

"Ones?"

"For the jukebox."

"The jukebox?"

The sun had just come up. It was early for Jonathan who often turned in with the rising sun rather than wake with it. Bathed and somewhat presentable, he confidently strode the busy Monday morning streets, reading the classified section of a local newspaper and searching for an address. He turned down an alley and stopped in front of a brick-faced office building. He stared at the entrance a moment before entering. A well-dressed, businesswoman greeted him in the building's lobby. She studied his unique choice of apparel.

"I'm interested in the job you have listed," he said, pointing to the San Francisco Chronicle in his hand.

The woman continued to study Jonathan before answering.

"The job's been filled. Sorry."

He stared at her for a few seconds. She didn't blink or look away. He then nodded before stepping back into the crowded street. He again scanned the classifieds, picked another job listing, and looked up to the street sign to determine what direction he needed to go next.

He walked or bussed to six other places that had advertised job openings he thought he might be able to land as well as perform. But at the same time, he was realistic. He knew getting a good job with little experience and no advanced degree or skill set was slim at best.

He struck out at all six places. At the first place, he was chased out of the building by a security guard before even getting a chance to talk to someone. At four other places, he filled out employment applications that were all about the same. In each case, he had to leave many of the sections incomplete because he had neither the experience nor the qualifications. At the last place, he sat with 12 other people in the waiting room. After a nearly two-hour wait with the same group of people, he finally got up and left.

The king bed rocked. The headboard bumped and banged the wall, shaking the pictures above the bed. Wearing only a slinky negligee, Katherine rode William hard. Both of her hands forcefully pressed down on his chest. He spied the clock on the nightstand, knowing he'd be late for the clinic again. These regular, early morning love-making sessions were fun and all, but they had started to affect his work. As she romped over his splayed-out body as if it were a playground jungle gym, he tried to slide out from under her.

"I can't be late three days in a row."

She stopped moving and sat on his bare chest, staring at him.

"Sorry, babe," he apologized.

He tried to move. She wouldn't let him, not budging from her position atop him.

"You promised me weeks ago that you'd cut back on your hours."

"We just sent out the job listing for another doc."

Without expression, she glared at him for a few moments before sliding off him.

Jonathan was up early again. It was Friday. He had tried to get a job for four straight days with no luck. But he wasn't ready to give up. Wearing a wrinkled tie, he sat by himself at the bar in the Tam, sipping a coffee in a to-go cup. He fingered an empty shot glass and called out to the morning bartender.

"I need one for the road."

The bartender, an older gentleman with gray hair and a noticeable limp, slowly shuffled over, carrying a bottle of Irish whiskey. He filled the shot glass in front of Jonathan who nodded and dumped the shot in the coffee.

"Put it on my tab."

"You don't have a tab."

Jonathan saluted the bartender, grabbed his spiked coffee, and dashed out the door. The bartender wiped the counter and shook his head.

Jonathan entered a small, mostly empty office. It was his first stop of the day. A dumpy, sloppily dressed bald man spun around on his stool behind a steel desk as Jonathan stepped into the room.

"I'm looking for a job."

"You've come to the right place."

"What type of job is it?"

"Sales. Do you have sales experience?"

"I can sell anything."

"What about office equipment?"

"Office equipment?"

"Copiers, fax machines, telephones, pagers, you know."

"I can sell the shit out of that stuff."

"When can you start?"

Jonathan started selling office equipment the following Monday. He was up before daylight and ready to go, carrying a folder full of brochures, listings of potential sales leads, and a handful of business cards with his name scribbled on them. But it rained. He stood under the awning at the entrance of his apartment building, gazing up to the low-hanging, heavy clouds. He eventually stepped into the sheets of rain. He had no umbrella, or the cash to spend on one, and was getting wet.

Although he held his folder over his head, he was soaked as he squeaked down a tiled hallway of an office building he was instructed to visit. He was greeted by an office manager who politely smiled but shook his head. That scene was repeated several more times that day. In nearly all the visits, the workers or managers at those places were quick to point out that their offices were already well-equipped and stocked with all the items he tried to sell.

Cold, tired, and still on foot, Jonathan reached the same coffee shop that Katherine often visited. The heavier rain from earlier had been replaced by a light but steady drizzle. Entering the place, he glanced around as if looking for someone. His clothes were damp. He had walked more than ten miles that day, covering several downtown blocks while trying his best to visit all the leads he had been given. He spent the last of his modest advance from his boss on a much-needed coffee.

He sipped the coffee slowly, wanting it to last, and took out a sales report form from a folder. The form was a little soggy after spending a good portion of the day in the rain. Under the heading for Monday, he filled in zeros under each category: copiers, fax machines, telephones, scanners, printers, and pagers. Each of the next three days, he would end up at the same coffee shop at the same time. He had not made a sale. The sales report for that first week was covered with zeros.

Jonathan was back on the streets early Friday morning, searching for a sale. Clumsily, but enthusiastically and a little desperate, he entered an office. He was greeted by a smiling young woman behind a desk.

"Can I speak with your office manager?"

"He's out," she said. "Is there something I can do?"

"I can think of a lot of things," he flirted.

She grinned and studied Jonathan, kicking her bare, crossed leg. He handed her his card and pulled out a brochure.

I'm trying to push some product."

"How's business?" she asked, taking the brochure and glancing at it.

"I need a sale in a bad way."

She stood and came out from behind the desk.

"I don't know if I can help you."

He followed her to a closed door. She opened it and clicked on the light. They entered. The room was full of every kind of office equipment that was available.

"Are you sure? I really, really need a sale."

"I'm sorry," she shrugged, nearly apologizing.

They stared a minute before she led him to the office entrance.

"You have my card."

She nodded as he exited. After the door closed behind him, she started to toss the brochure and business card into a trash can. Jonathan suddenly re-entered the office.

"Oh, by the way," he informed her with much enthusiasm. "I forgot to mention ..."

His voice trailed off as he watched her throw the card and brochure away.

"New customers get a 25-percent discount on initial orders," he mumbled.

The enthusiasm was gone. They stared a moment. She looked away. He nodded, then left. She reached into the trash can, retrieved the card, and placed it on her desk.

Not in the mood to finish the day, Jonathan walked to the coffee shop earlier than normal. He sipped coffee and filled out the sales report form for the final day of the week. He wrote Friday on the top and entered zeros under each category, just as he had the previous days. He also added at the top of the form on that day several other categories -- meals, bank deposits, beer, whiskey shots, and blow jobs. He entered zeros under each of those categories as well. Suddenly sensing someone standing over him, he looked up. Katherine was behind him.

"What are you doing here?"

"Just finishing up some paperwork," he proudly announced. "Sales report, you know. I'm a working man, now."

"What do you sell?"

"Office equipment."

"How's it going?"

"Busy," he answered, sliding his arm over the report, trying to hide the truth. "It's been unbelievable."

"Is this what you want?"

He didn't answer as they stared. She motioned to a table with her friends and continued to study him.

"I have to go."

"I'm sorry," he apologized before she could walk away. "I did lie to you in the park, but I didn't take your wallet."

"Please don't come here anymore."

"Katherine, wait."

She briefly closed her eyes but walked away and joined her friends at another table. Loosening his tie, he slowly finished his coffee and watched as she chatted with her friends. Not once in the 20 minutes after she had arrived did she look at him. He glanced down to the sales report on the table, and, without hesitation, crumbled it into a ball, and tossed it in the trash as he left the shop.

After he walked out, he angrily threw the folder of brochures and business cards into the first garbage can he passed. He took one last look at Katherine in the front window, pulled off his tie, and threw it into the next garbage can. As he strode up the street, Katherine finally looked away from her friends and watched him. Her friends talked to her, but for that short time, she didn't hear a word they were saying.

Jonathan approached his apartment. Before he could get to the door, he noticed his belongings had been pushed into several piles outside in the hallway. He stepped over and through the mess and tried to unlock the apartment door with his key. The key no longer worked. Exhausted from what had been a wasted week, he took a seat among all the things he owned, knowing he had nowhere to go. He was homeless.

Chapter Eight
Nobody Was Supposed to Fall in Love.

The sun had yet to rise. William stared at himself in the mirror as he adjusted the tie around his neck. He looked exhausted. Katherine appeared behind him and wrapped her arms around his chest.

"I hate when you're on call."

"Not as much as I do," he said, not taking his eyes from the reflection of himself in the mirror.

"That's up for debate," she said.

He brushed his hair and checked his appearance, still not looking at her.

"Stay a little longer. I'm not feeling well."

He turned and pecked her on the cheek. She released her arms from him when he didn't respond.

"Just hold me, William. They won't miss you for an hour or two."

He checked his appearance one last time.

"You'll be there all night and most of tomorrow."

"Don't forget about the reception tomorrow evening," he reminded her, while searching for his white coat.

She closely watched him until he found it and started to leave the room.

"How's the search for the new doctor going?"

He hesitated at the doorway and turned.

"These things take time."

"It's been nearly two months."

"We have some interviews scheduled."

He wouldn't look at her. She nodded as he slung the white coat over his shoulder and left the room. She always knew when he lied to her. After she heard the garage door close, she reluctantly slid back into bed. She wanted rest but knew sleep would be difficult because she had been feeling ill most mornings. And she especially was growing tired of being left alone.

In the darkness, Jonathan slept on a musty and decomposing wrestling mat in the back of the damp and deserted boxing gym. The place had been for sale since Charlie had died. The entire space had been cleared out, and the electricity and water had long been shut off. Nobody knew that Jonathan had a key to a backdoor. He had been living there for several weeks after getting kicked out of his apartment. As long as the building was on the market, he planned to sleep there. He had no other place to go and little money to rent something different.

An alarm from an old wind-up clock rattled him from a deep sleep. He slammed the alarm off, wishing to sleep a few more hours but knowing he couldn't. Under the cover of darkness so as not to be seen, he would enter the building late at night and exit early in the morning before the sun came up. The accommodations weren't much, but it was significantly better sleeping behind a locked door with a roof over his head than out in the streets.

He had lived most of his adult life alone and had grown to accept it. But the loneliness he felt that morning was extra heavy. Pulling a toothbrush from his backpack, he loaded it with fresh toothpaste from a small tube and brushed his mouth clean. He rinsed with distilled water from a plastic jug and spit into the opening of a drain in the middle of the cracked concrete floor. It was payday. He had to take a bus across town to pick up a small but meaningful paycheck. A past acquaintance had hooked him up with a job cleaning sidewalks, trimming grass, and emptying trash cans near the Embarcadero. He was off for a couple of days and hadn't had a drink in weeks. He was looking forward to blowing a few bucks and wasting an afternoon at the Tam later.

It was a beautiful sunny day. Morning had slowly crept into afternoon. The house was quiet. As usual, nothing was worth watching on television. Like the previous days before, Katherine had been feeling a little weak, nauseated, and light-headed and hadn't left the house. But that day, she also was restless and bored. She didn't need to clean. She had taken care of that earlier in the week. Her friends also were busy. Instead, she sat on her bedroom floor by the clothes hamper, separating the dirty clothes into piles. But the piles were quite small as William had been at the clinic for most of the week and hadn't been home to dirty any clothes. There wasn't much of anything to wash. As she reached deep into the hamper, she noticed something on the bottom. She pulled it out and studied it a moment. It was Jonathan's black leather motorcycle jacket. She had forgotten she still had it.

After picking up his paycheck, Jonathan locked himself in the bathroom of a convenience store he often visited and took off his shirt. He pulled a bar of soap that had been wrapped in a napkin from his backpack and turned on the sink faucet. Wetting the soap, he lathered up his hands before applying the soap to his bare arms, back, and chest. He then leaned his head under the cold, running water to wet his mop of hair. Again, he lathered up his hands and covered his face and entire head with the soap. For the next several minutes, he tried his best to rinse and wipe the soap from his upper body and hair with water from the sink. He then dried himself with handfuls of paper towels.

Carrying the leather motorcycle jacket, Katherine topped the creaky steps. Still feeling weak, she briefly rested a moment to catch her breath before walking down the hallway to the door of Jonathan's old apartment. Not knowing he hadn't lived there for weeks, she took a deep breath before knocking on the door. She felt nervous about seeing him again but didn't understand why. After a short wait, the door opened. To her surprise, a rather large, shirtless man appeared. He had an enormous belly and a barrel chest that was covered with wisps of curly gray hair.

"Is Jonathan here?"

"He don't live here no more."

"Do you know when he moved out?"

"I've been here a month."

"You wouldn't happen to know where he is now?"

"Nope," he said with a shrug. "You're the third or fourth person who's stopped, askin' for him."

The Tam was extremely busy. It was Friday. The jukebox roared, and the drinks flowed. Jonathan pushed open the door, filling the entrance of the dark bar with much-needed sunlight. He paused a moment until most everyone looked over to him, then stepped into the bar. A cheer rang out. Laughing, he raised his arms and pumped his fists, like a returning sports hero after a great victory. He had badly missed his old home and friends.

His favorite blonde bartender smiled and pushed to him a shot glass full of tequila. Without hesitation, he drained it and slid the empty glass forward, motioning for a refill.

"Where've you been?" she asked over the noise and commotion of the bar, pouring him another tequila.

"Trying to earn a few bucks. Get back on my feet," he said. "I got kicked out of my place several weeks ago."

"Yeah, I heard. Ted went to check on you. We were worried."

He lifted the shot glass of tequila.

"You having one?"

She reached for another shot glass and filled it. They touched the glasses and knocked back the shots.

"And keep 'em coming. I don't have anywhere to be until tomorrow morning," he said, tossing two $20 bills on the bar. "Is my bike still parked in back?"

"Yeah, Ted's been riding it."

"You'd think with all the money he makes here in this palace he could buy his own motorcycle."

"He loses money on this dump."

"How's that?" Jonathan asked. "Look at it in here. It's beautiful."

"Because his best customers are guys like you."

"Like me?"

"Your thirst is bigger than your paycheck."

Jonathan and the bartender laughed. She poured him another tequila as he spun around on the barstool and glanced to the jukebox. One of his favorite songs, "*She Sang Amazing Grace*", by Jerry Lee Lewis, started to play as the bar's front door opened. Katherine stood in the entranceway. She spotted Jonathan and hesitated before joining him at the bar on the barstool next to him.

"I thought you were a salesman?"

"I took the afternoon off."

"I forgot I had this," she said, holding out his leather jacket.

"I wondered where that was," he said, taking the jacket. "How'd you find me?"

"It wasn't very hard."

"Tequila?"

"I'm running late," she shook her head. "I need to pick up your parents."

"For what?"

"We're going to a reception later for William. He's getting an award from the city for his charity work."

"Sounds like a blast," Jonathan sarcastically remarked. "Come on, hang out. You'll have more fun here, with me."

"I can't."

"How 'bout a coffee sometime?"

"I can't," she said as they stared. "I've got to go. I just wanted to bring your jacket ..."

"Bullshit," he interrupted. "You didn't come all this way …"

"I have to go. You got your jacket."

They continued to study each other. Jonathan didn't say anything. He could only grit his teeth.

"Goodbye, Jonathan."

She quickly turned and disappeared through the door. With a faraway look in his eyes, he watched her walk away.

"You, OK?" the bartender asked.

"I had almost forgotten about her. Why'd she have to show up here today? My day off."

"Sister, right?"

"Sister-in-law," he said, continuing to stare at the door.

"Whatever. That's not how a sister-in-law looks at her brother-in-law," the bartender said as he grabbed his jacket and hopped off the barstool. "Where you going?"

"To straighten out a family matter. Give me the keys to my bike."

Sandra, Jonathan's mother, waited inside her house and watched for Katherine from the front door window. Katherine's sporty new, black Mercedes coupe finally pulled into the driveway. Sandra opened the front door and stepped outside as Katherine approached.

"You're not ready?" Sandra said, leading Katherine inside the house.

"I know. I know. I'm running late."

"Ray," Sandra called. "Katherine's here."

"Do you have the pictures William wanted for the reception?"

"In that box," Sandra pointed, "there on the table."

Katherine picked up the stack of pictures. There was a book under them. She stared at the book.

"That's Jonathan's high school yearbook," she said as Katherine opened it and flipped through the pages. "What a shame that he never got to graduate."

"What was that?" Katherine asked.

Sandra turned and grabbed her jacket.

"I'm ready. Let's go."

"No, what did you say?"

"I'm ready to go."

"No, before that? About Jonathan?" she asked as Sandra didn't respond. "Jonathan never finished high school, did he?"

Sandra shook her head.

"Why did you tell me before that he did?"

"Everyone graduates from high school," she whispered. "He's a bright boy. He was top of his class. She never should have dropped out."

"You were embarrassed, weren't you?" Katherine asked as Sandra looked away. "What really happened to Jonathan?"

"He wouldn't listen to me or his father. He dropped out of school …," she paused. "As a mother, I am not supposed to say this, but …"

"But what?"

"I always knew William would be successful. I never worried about him. But Jonathan …," she stopped herself again, shook her head, and looked away.

"What about Jonathan?"

"Jonathan was different."

"What are you not supposed to say?"

"Jonathan was my favorite," Sandra confessed as Ray entered the room.

"So, did he drop out of life because of a girlfriend?"

"That was part of it. And …," she said, glancing at Ray who shook his head, and interrupted herself. "But that was such a long time ago."

Holding a box of pictures, Katherine entered the bedroom in a rush. William flipped through several sport jackets of different styles and colors as he got ready. She placed the pictures on the bed and stared at William until he looked over.

"How was clinic?"

"Chaos as usual."

He looked at her as she sat on the bed.

"Come on, you need to get ready."

"Do I really have to go? I haven't been feeling well lately. I'm so tired right now."

"Nobody's as tired as I am," he said without a hint of care or concern for her. "And besides, it wouldn't look good for the 'man of the hour' to show up alone."

She glanced away before stepping into the closet to pick out an outfit and started to undress.

"We're running late, you know," he reminded her. "Did you get my parents?"

"They're downstairs."

"We'll be in the car," he said, grabbing the box of pictures. "Please hurry."

Jonathan rode the motorcycle into his parents' driveway and squealed to a stop. He shut off the bike engine and hopped off. He glanced around as he approached the front door, knocking a couple of times and ringing the doorbell. There was no answer. He turned the knob of the front door. It was locked. He flashed a peek over his shoulder to check if anyone was watching. He then bent his arm and broke the glass of the door with a single, forceful jab of his elbow. He quickly reached in through the broken window and unlocked the door. Unknown to him, a neighbor spied from their living room window from across the street and dialed a phone.

Jonathan rushed from room to room, rummaging through papers in stacks on different tables in the house. In the kitchen, he spotted an invitation under a magnet stuck to the refrigerator door. He studied it a moment before stuffing it in his coat pocket. Before leaving the room, he noticed the yearbook on the table. He stopped, picked it up, and flipped through it until he found his own picture. As he stared at the clean-cut image of himself, a car drove in the driveway and parked behind his motorcycle. He glanced out the window. It was a police squad car.

"Shit."

Jonathan ducked and waited by a side door off the kitchen. Once the two cops got out of their car and approached the front door of the house, he dashed out the side door, running to the bike and hopping on. The cops immediately spotted him and sprinted in his direction as he kickstarted the bike. Before they could reach him, he wheeled the motorcycle around and sped by them through his parents' front lawn, kicking up large divots of grass and dirt high into the air behind the bike. The cops scrambled for their car before getting in and chasing after the speeding motorcycle.

In a downtown building close to city hall, a crowd of more than 200 people, including many top San Francisco dignitaries, had gathered in a reception hall. A six-piece jazz band softly played. The guests enjoyed wine, sampled finger foods, and exchanged pleasantries. Circled by friends, family, and colleagues, William easily joked and conversed with his admirers. Katherine was nowhere to be seen. She was in a lady's room stall where she had been vomiting for most of the time since she arrived at the reception.

On the other side of the city, Jonathan led the police on a wild chase. He raced the motorcycle across neighborhood yards, down alleyways, and even busted through a white picket fence. But he couldn't lose them. With tires squealing around every turn, the cop car stayed close behind him.

In the reception hall, all the guests were seated. The program had started. At the front, William stood at a podium and addressed the group by telling a story from his medical school days. Katherine was seated in the front row with William's parents on one side of her and the mayor of the city on the other.

"It was my surgery rotation," William recalled. "I had been awake for days on call, exhausted. I was helping with a heart transplant. The attending surgeon actually handed me the heart that was to be transplanted."

The members of the audience intently listened.

"Hold it as still as you can," William continued. "Do not let anything happen to it. I held that heart out in front of me with both hands as still as I could."

He briefly paused and glanced around the room, before continuing with the story.

"I was so very tired. And I was standing so still and so calm. I literally fell asleep on my feet."

The audience laughed.

"The attending surgeon had to wake me. 'You did a great job, Hayes' he said, gently prying the heart from my hands. 'You'll make a fine surgeon one day'. And that, my friends, is how I ended up in pediatrics."

The audience laughed louder, before applauding.

Nearing downtown, Jonathan, still on the motorcycle, appeared with a roar from a side street behind an apartment building. He raced down a steep section of Steiner Street. A second police car had joined the chase. The two squad cars wheeled around a turn and pulled closer behind him. Approaching an intersection with a red light at the bottom of a hill, Jonathan revved the bike faster and zipped through a busy four-way stop, barely squeezing between a moving pickup truck and a crowded city bus. Sirens and car horns blared. He quickly glanced back over his shoulder. The first police car slammed on the brakes and slid sideways, ramming the bus. The second police car crashed into the first one.

With the bike idling, Jonathan held the invitation he took from his mother's kitchen and studied the buildings that lined a busy downtown street near city hall, searching for an address number. He checked over his shoulder after hearing sirens in the distance. He revved the engine a couple of times and circled the bike around onto the sidewalk, before aiming it at the entrance of a specific building. Without hesitation, he suddenly gunned the bike and zoomed up the two sets of steep concrete stairs in front of the building at a high rate of speed. In a matter of seconds, the motorcycle burst through the glass front doors, and continued down a long, tiled hallway before violently crashing through the closed, wooden double-doors of a large reception hall.

Chaos followed. Pieces of jagged, splintered wood hurled through the air. A cloud of dust reduced visibility. People yelled and screamed. They ran to the other side of the reception hall in the opposite direction of where the bike crashed into the room. The sound of sirens grew louder. Jonathan had managed to stay on the smoking bike that had stalled. He quickly scanned the room as if searching for someone.

As the dust cleared and the screams died down, he continued to glance around the room. He suddenly realized that he had crashed a wedding reception. A furious young woman in a wedding gown stomped towards him, shouting obscenities.

"Sorry, wrong party," he said with a shrug.

Police sirens blared louder. Guests from the reception for William in the room next door rushed into the damaged hall. Still on the bike, Jonathan first spotted William, then his mother.

"Jonathan!" She shouted in both disbelief and horror.

He ignored her, frantically scanning the crowd. He finally located Katherine. They stared at each other for a moment.

"Get on!" He shouted as she showed him a puzzled look but didn't say a word or step closer to him. "Hurry! Get on! We have to go!"

The sirens were more persistent and howled louder. The authorities were close. He tried to kick start the bike. It wouldn't start. A puddle of engine fluid covered the floor around it. Suddenly, a gang of cops rushed into the room. He again looked at Katherine.

"No one was supposed to fall in love," he said.

She looked at him sympathetically. He glanced at his mother who cried as the cops descended on him. The officers aggressively wrestled Jonathan off the bike and forcefully threw him to the floor. In the scrum, he fought and struggled as they violently punched, elbowed, and kicked him. Eventually, the cops secured a pair of handcuffs around his wrists. His mother wailed during the entire fracas. Katherine couldn't watch. She quickly left the room. William didn't follow her. Instead, he stayed behind and watched as his brother was viciously beaten, before being hauled away.

Chapter Nine

I Drove a Motorcycle Through a Wall to Be with You.

It was early morning. Alone, Katherine studied the results of an over-the-counter home pregnancy test strip that she had picked up at the drug store. She glanced at the directions on the product information sheet and examined the strip again. She took a deep breath and opened the package of a different pregnancy test kit from another company. She repeated the test and checked the results. After the test, she bagged up all the packaging, strips, and information that came with the kits, before dialing a number.

Wearing a hospital gown, she sat by herself in the doctor's examination room. The door slowly pushed opened, and her doctor and a nurse entered.

"Congratulations, Katherine!" the doctor's voice boomed as she sighed. "You're 100 percent pregnant! But you knew that, right?"

"Yes."

"Have you told Bill the news?"

"Not yet," she shook her head. "I wanted to be sure."

"You two will make wonderful parents."

"Yes," she said but glancing away.

"Give Bill my regards."

"I will."

"Your husband's the best."

She politely nodded.

After her appointment, Katherine entered the bustling county jail. She waited for a few minutes at the front desk until the desk cop acknowledged her.

"I'm here for Jonathan Hayes."

"Hayes?" the cop asked with a puzzled look. "Are you his lawyer? What would you want with him?"

"Is he here or not?" she asked again, not responding to his question.

"Yeah, yeah, he's always here."

"I want to bail him out," she said, pulling a pen and checkbook from her purse.

"You're throwin' your money away."

"How much?" she asked, holding the pen to a blank check. He didn't answer. She glanced up at him. "How much?"

Jonathan sat on a cot in his jail cell, staring at the floor. A tray of uneaten food was next to him. He had a black eye along with several scratches and bruises on his face. A cop entered and opened the cell door. Jonathan looked up.

"I can't believe it. Someone actually paid your bond."

Katherine and Jonathan shared a table in her regular coffee shop. He looked ragged and exhausted. With a concerned gaze, she stared at him from across the table. He avoided eye contact with her. Neither said a word for several minutes. Finally, Katherine pulled a sheet of paper from her purse and started to read it.

"They've dropped the breaking and entering charge, but not reckless driving, reckless endangerment, destruction of public property, disobeying an officer …," she stopped and looked up. "It goes on and on."

He didn't respond and still wouldn't look at her.

"And probation from a previous charge."

He didn't react, continuing to stare into his coffee.

"William's lawyer thinks it'll be impossible for you to avoid jail time."

"William's lawyer?" He snapped. "What the hell does he know?"

"He's willing to represent you at no cost."

"I don't need charity from anyone, especially Billy and his fucking lawyer."

There was a short pause.

"What were you thinking?"

"I was desperate."

"Desperate?"

"I didn't know what else to do. Charlie had just died. You walked out of my life."

"I was never in your life," she shot back, before pausing a moment. "So, you were expecting me to hop on the bike, ride off with you, and leave my husband in front of his family, friends, and colleagues?"

"Just like in the movies," he said with a slight smile.

"And you thought I'd go with you?"

"Yeah," he answered confidently.

"We hardly know each other."

"It's the way you look at me."

"This isn't the movies," she said.

"Don't waste your life," he said, changing the subject.

"I'm sorry I didn't believe you, except …"

"What I lied about?" he asked, interrupting her. "It was Billy."

"What about him?"

"He had it all. Why did he steal from me the only thing that mattered? To come home and find him in bed with my girlfriend. My own fucking brother. Girlfriends may come and go, but not brothers," he said, briefly pausing. "It wasn't the girl who ruined my life. I looked up to him. I did all I could from jumping off a bridge that night."

"Is your interest in me then payback for what William did to you?"

"I drove a motorcycle through a wall to be with you."

They studied each other. Neither said a word for a couple of minutes.

"And now …," she started to say.

"And now, I'm in big trouble," he interrupted her. "I know. I've been to jail before."

"What are you going to do?"

"I don't know."

She shook her head and checked her watch.

"I need to leave. I must meet William. Do you want a ride somewhere?"

"Where would I go?"

"I just can't leave you here."

"I'll be all right. This is nothing new for me."

"Here," she said, pulling some cash from her purse and extending it to him.

"I don't want your money."

"Take it. You need to eat."

He reluctantly took the money as she stood. They studied each other for a moment before she turned and headed for the door.

"Katie," he called out. "I didn't take your wallet. You know that."

She quickly left without turning.

Feeling chilled and feverish, Katherine watched William from under the covers of their bed as he got ready for work. She also was nauseated and cramping. Her head, lower back and belly ached. She had so little energy she wondered if she could even get out of bed that morning. In his haste, William hurried out of the room with neither a kiss nor a word of goodbye. She had yet to tell him about the pregnancy. It had been more than a month since she found out. So, instead of feelings of joy and excitement, she felt guilt and sadness. Never had she been so alone.

Suddenly sensing the need to vomit, she struggled out of bed and dragged herself to the bathroom. She forcefully and violently vomited the full contents of her gut before dry heaving off and on for nearly an hour. The stabbing pains and cramps in her belly intensified. With the little strength she had left, she pulled herself up onto the commode seat and spent the better part of the morning there. Before leaving the bathroom, she regrettably glanced into the toilet. It was filled with blood and other discharges. She had lost the baby.

Chapter Ten
I Want to Feel That Way Again.

Wearing hospital scrubs, a disheveled and obviously tipsy William entered the country club bar. His hair was messed. His face was flushed. He was unsteady on his feet. Jessica was bartending. She had only one other customer at the time- a wrinkled but distinguished-looking, white-haired gentleman who could barely keep his eyes open. It was near closing time. William awkwardly took a seat at the bar, smiling at Jessica.

"Where you've been?" she asked, holding up a bottle of gin.

"At the clinic," he nodded. "I haven't slept in a couple of days."

"Or bathed. I can smell you from here," she said, fixing a gin and tonic. "By the way you stumbled in here, it looks like you've been to more than just the clinic."

"I hit a few places on my way over here."

Jessica slid him the drink and glanced to the clock.

"I'll be closing up soon."

William drank the cocktail in one large gulp.

"You better make the next one a double then."

As she started to make the second drink, he slowly dropped his head forward as if falling asleep.

"You going to be OK, Bill?"

"You got anything to eat back there?"

"The kitchen closed at 10," she said, setting the double gin and tonic in front of him. "I have a half of a turkey sandwich in the back I didn't finish earlier."

"I can't eat your food."

She briefly disappeared into the kitchen and quickly returned with a Styrofoam container.

"Please eat," she said, opening the containing and placing it in front of him.

William initially stared at the food, before glancing up to her.

"Eat it."

He took a bite of the sandwich. She laughed, watching him eat.

"You're pathetic."

He didn't look up as he focused on finishing the half of a sandwich in his hands.

"How are you getting home? You can't drive like this."

"What do you have in mind?" he asked, glancing up from the sandwich with a sneaky grin.

"Let me call you a cab."

"What are you doing after you get out of here?"

"I'm going home."

"It's too early to go home," he said, swallowing the last of the sandwich and taking a large drink of the cocktail. "You wouldn't want to …"

"I don't do married men," she interrupted.

"Let's get a drink. I'll take you any place you want to go. Let me change. We'll drive into the city."

"Not interested."

"Or we could stay around here. Walk the golf course. Check out the stars. It's a beautiful night."

"Call your wife. She may be in that."

"Come on. You've always treated me different from the other guys here. Let's hang out. All the flirting- the winks, the secret smiles when no one else is watching, rubbing my shoulder, touching my hand," he said, before motioning to the empty leftover food container. "Giving me your midnight snack."

She looked disappointed and turned away from him, putting the cash from the register into a bank deposit bag.

"Why so friendly? I thought there was a little more …"

"They don't pay me much by the hour here," she again interrupted, turning to him. "I survive on tips."

"So?"

"So, it pays to be friendly. It helps with the bills."

"But I notice how you look at me."

"Surely, you're not that naïve."

"What if I weren't married?"

"But you are."

"Let's pretend I'm not."

"That's impossible."

"Why?"

"You're the type that'll always be married."

"Type?"

"Finish your drink. I'm closing."

She turned and shook the old fellow's arm who was sleeping at the bar.

"Hey, Mr. Cartwright."

The old man struggled to open his eyes and glanced around, appearing somewhat confused.

"It's time to go."

The old man rubbed his bloodshot eyes.

"You need a ride?" she asked as he nodded.

"I'll take a ride," Bill called out.

"We'll go as soon as *Bill's* cab gets here."

William awkwardly pounced into bed next to Katherine as she slept. The stench of booze, body odor, and hospital antiseptic overwhelmed the room. He had just gotten home after the hectic 60-hour shift at the clinic and the three-stop pub hop before closing the country club bar. Not ready for sleep and horned up from multiple gin and tonics and his encounter with Jessica, he crawled on top of Katherine, looking for sex, like he often did after a long shift. Waking, she instantly turned away. He stretched a hand stained with betadine under the covers and grabbed at her panties, pulling them halfway down her thighs. Initially, she tried to resist. With his knee, he nudged her legs apart and positioned himself to mount her.

"No," she said, pushing at his chest. "Not tonight."

"Come on, baby, I miss you," he slurred; his sour breath reeked of the smell of juniper. "What happened to that sex-crazed chick who'd make me late for work?"

"Not now," she mumbled, struggling to free herself. "I don't feel well."

Pinned underneath him, nearly paralyzed, she was too exhausted to push him off and too numb to care. Excitedly, he mounted her. She closed her eyes. She felt nothing. He moaned, groaned, and thrust into her, seemingly having the time of his life. For the briefest time, he was the happiest man on earth- and she the loneliest. Luckily for her, he lacked stamina and came quickly. His deep gasps of satisfaction blew hollow in her ear. Beads of sweat dripped from his hair and fell from the tip of his nose into her eyes. Spent, he grinned, not for Katherine, but for himself, and rolled off her. Wiping the salty perspiration from her eyes, she immediately leaped out of bed and dashed into the bathroom, locking the door behind her. Finally catching his breath, he quickly fell asleep to the sound of the running water from the shower.

William and Katherine attended a member appreciation reception in the grand ballroom of the country club. He wore a tuxedo and she a shimmering sequined blue evening gown. She looked spectacular, but he hardly noticed. He easily laughed and joked with other couples as they moved about the crowded ballroom. Katherine, on the other hand, said little as she lagged behind him, pretending her best to smile. Months had passed since the miscarriage, and she never said a word to anyone. She had mostly isolated herself from family and friends, hiding away in her big, empty house. William still worked long hours at the clinic and spent a good portion of his free time at the country club. She couldn't hide her disinterest in the reception. It was the last place she wanted to be.

Out of the crowd, Jessica appeared, carrying a tray of glass flutes filled with champagne. She tried to avoid William but couldn't as he reached for two champagnes when she approached. Once he took the champagnes, she abruptly turned away from him without making eye contact or saying a word. Instead of handing one of the drinks to Katherine, William stood and stared at Jessica as she walked away.

"What's the matter?" Katherine asked, studying her suddenly distracted husband.

He handed Katherine one of the champagnes without responding or looking at her and followed Jessica into the crowd, leaving Katherine to stand alone. William slowly approached Jessica, watching her hand out the drinks she carried. Once the tray was empty, William stepped in her path.

"Where you been?" he asked her. "I haven't seen you in weeks. I've been looking for you."

"I needed a break from this place," she said.

"Was it something I said?"

"I'm working," she replied, holding up her empty.

"I've been wanting to apologize."

"They need me in the kitchen. I can't talk."

"I may have been a little too forward that one late night weeks ago."

"It's OK," she said, glancing around the buzzing ballroom. "It's over."

"It was the booze. An empty stomach. And I hadn't slept …"

"I don't want to talk about it," she interrupted.

"That wasn't me."

"I have to refill my tray," she said, appearing frustrated. "I have to go."

As she started to walk away, he placed his hand on her shoulder. She immediately stopped and pulled away from him.

"That wasn't me that night," he repeated but with more conviction.

"That was exactly who you are," she said in a quiet but firm tone, leaning her face closer to his. "One thing I've learned after working here is that no one is more honest than the drunkest man in the room. And you *were* that man the other night."

"Jessica, but …"

She quickly turned and stomped away as Katherine, who had been watching the awkward exchange, appeared. William turned to her.

"Get me out of here," she said. "I can't stand to be here another minute."

It was a quiet ride home. Neither said a word during the drive. Katherine locked herself in their bedroom, and William slept on the couch in the living room. He was extremely angry he had to leave the reception early. It was usually one of his favorite nights of the year at the country club. Katherine was furious. She tossed and turned most of the night and slept but only a few hours. William woke her the next morning by pounding on the door to the bedroom. He needed to get in there and get ready for work. Not looking at him, Katherine unlocked the door and returned to the bed, hiding herself under the covers.

"Can you *please* try and enjoy yourself at the club next time?" he snapped as he dressed for the clinic. "Those were my friends last night. You hardly said a word the entire time we were there, which wasn't very long I'd like to remind you."

"Maybe you could show me as much attention as you did the cocktail girl."

"Jesus Christ."

"She didn't seem so happy with you. What'd you do to her?"

"I hardly know her," he mumbled.

"What'd you do to her? She seemed pretty pissed off about something."

"There's nothing going on."

"Is she the reason you're always running off to the club?" Katherine asked as he turned to the mirror to adjust his tie. "I stupidly thought it was the golf."

"Give me a break, Katherine."

"No. No. I want to know what's going on," she hollered, sitting up in bed. "You don't get it. I just want to be alone with you. That's all. Spend some time together. Is that too much to ask?"

"Nothing's going on."

"Then, why do you want to be anywhere else but here with me?"

"That's not true."

"And I *know*," she shouted, getting out of bed. "You'd rather be at the clinic than at home."

"Bullshit."

"Don't lie to me. No one needs to work that many hours. We certainly don't need the money right now."

There was a short pause as he finished getting ready.

"What's wrong with you?" he asked, turning to her. "You haven't been yourself lately."

"And you still haven't cut back on your hours. How long's it been now?" she asked, studying him. "I don't think you want to."

"Is this some kind of hormonal thing you're going through?" He asked, glancing away and checking his appearance in a mirror.

"Fuck you."

He angrily turned to her. They stared a moment.

"I'll see you in a couple of days," he grumbled, before storming out of the room.

Gray clouds lingered in the skies over the secured yard of the county jail. The inmates were allowed outside for one hour each day after lunch. Most of the inmates took advantage of the opportunity for physical activity. Jonathan only went outside once or twice a week. When he did, he usually sat alone off to the side and never participated in any of the activities, such as basketball, volleyball, or ping pong. He didn't mingle much with the other prisoners, preferring to be left to himself.

On that day as he sat alone on a wooden picnic table in the yard, a loud siren sounded. That was a warning signal for all the inmates to immediately take a seat and not to move from that spot. As the siren continued to blare, the director of corrections at the facility, accompanied by two guards, entered the yard and approached Jonathan.

"Hayes?" he called out.

He motioned to Jonathan that it was all right to stand.

"Yes, sir?" Jonathan stood.

"I guess the county is short on beds. Because you've never been a troublemaker here and seeing that we don't have many free ones to give 'em, I've offered to have your sentence reduced."

"Reduced?"

"I'll try to get you out of here in the next week or two."

"But it's only been eight months."

"Exactly," the director said, as they stared. "So, don't make me look bad. I don't want to see your dumb-ass face here ever again. You got that?"

"Yes, sir."

Katherine sat in the driver's seat of her Mercedes coupe in the parking lot of the county jail for several minutes. Her car was still running. She watched the entrance of the non-descript, guarded gray brick building. With a deep breath, she shut off the ignition and exited the Mercedes. Entering the jail, she was greeted by the front-desk officer who remembered her from a previous visit.

"Hayes, right?"

She nodded. The officer shook his head.

"He's requested no visitors."

"No visitors?"

"He won't even see his mother."

Katherine and the officer studied each other for a moment.

She turned, but before she could leave the officer called out, "They're lettin' him go next Friday. Four months early for good behavior."

"Good behavior?" she asked, walking back to him.

"It's a nice way of sayin' the jail is overcrowded with guys worse than him."

She nodded and reached out a small envelope.

"Can I leave this for him when he gets out?"

He took the envelope and filed it away. The officer turned and studied her before she could leave.

"I just don't get it."

"What's that?"

"Are you related to him?"

"I'm married to his brother."

"Then what is it about him that keeps bringin' you back?"

"He's part of the family."

132

"Why doesn't his brother ever visit?" he asked, as she shrugged. "I think there's more to it."

"Like I said, he's part of the family."

"He's small-time. Guys like him pass through here every day. He's a waste of time."

"You'll never know him like I do."

It was late afternoon. The house was quiet. As usual, Katherine was the only one home. She vacuumed and dusted a small room that William used as an office. After dusting, she reached under a desk and collected a small garbage can and a separate waste basket from under a shredder. She dumped the contents of each into a large trash bag. As the waste fell from the shredder basket into the bag, something caught her attention. With a puzzled look, she reached into the trash bag and pulled out what looked to be the remains of a shredded credit card. She peered into the bag before pulling out another shredded card.

Jonathan stood at the front desk of the county jail in civilian clothes. He was pale, much thinner, and had cut most of his hair off. Emotionless, he filled out and signed a stack of forms and documents in front of him.

"You got any questions?" the officer at the front desk asked.

"I've been through this before," he shook his head.

"You sure that was eight months?" the officer asked, handing Jonathan a large folder of personal items.

"Felt longer on the other side of the bars."

"All right," the officer said, taking the last form from Jonathan, "you're all set."

Before leaving, Jonathan dumped out the folder on the counter. He reached for a pair of sunglasses from the small pile of his belongings and placed them on the top of his forehead. As he sifted through the pile, a small envelope caught his attention. He opened it and pulled out the cable car keychain he had given Katherine.

"Will we be seein' you again?" the officer asked.

"Who knows?" Jonathan said, studying the keychain. "It depends on how desperate I get."

Katherine sat alone in the empty waiting room of an obstetrician's office. Because of the miscarriage, her doctor referred her to a colleague who specialized in fertility and difficult pregnancies. She stared at a magazine article on infant care but couldn't concentrate enough to read it. She was nervous. Unlike the first pregnancy, this one was an accident. The doctor visit was just a formality. As before, she knew what the result would be. As she thumbed through the pages of the magazine, a nurse entered.

"Ms. Hayes?" the nurse called as Katherine stood. "Will you please come with me? Round two, huh?"

With a nod, Katherine followed the nurse through a door that led down a long, sterile hallway. The nurse turned and commented in a quiet voice as if telling a secret.

"We've got good news for you and your husband."

Katherine forced an awkward smile.

With the engine running and the left-turn signal blinking, Katherine sat in the driver's seat of her car, stopped in the exit lane of the obstetrician's parking lot. Staring at her cell phone, she finally entered William's number but paused before canceling the call. She checked the rearview mirror, then the roadway, glancing to her left, then to the right. No cars were coming in either direction. She began to turn left but hesitated before changing course and making a sweeping right-hand turn. As she drove away, the left-turn indicator continued to blink.

Wearing his white lab coat, William entered the house. Tossing his keys on a table near the front door, he took a deep breath, seemingly happy to be home after a long 48-hour shift at the clinic. Exhausted, he walked into the dining room, poured himself a tall glass of bourbon, and called out.

"Katherine? Katherine?"

Sipping his drink, he walked through the kitchen and the living room. He stopped at the bottom of the stairs that led to the second floor. He called her name again.

"Katherine?"

There was still no answer. He passed by his office in the house and noticed that there was something on the desk. He entered the room and picked up the remnants of the shredded credit cards.

It was a bright day. Jonathan stepped out of the county jail, slipping the sunglasses over his eyes. He avoided going outside to the yard since finding out he was getting out jail early and hadn't seen sunlight for nearly two weeks. He had isolated himself in his cell. He didn't want anything or anyone to sabotage his early release. Before walking away, he lingered a moment outside the entrance and turned his face up to the warming rays of the midday sun, taking a deep breath of fresh air. Freedom had never felt or smelled so good.

Relieved to be released from confinement, he strolled down a street lined with acacias and fern pines. He allowed himself to study the cloudless blue sky above, and, for the first time, noticed planters and nearby gardens of blooming white lilies, yellow buttercups, and orange poppies. It was good to be free again, but the world looked different.

Although he didn't have anywhere to go, little money, and even fewer prospects for meaningful employment, he had hope. He badly missed the Tam, but he knew it was best to try to forget the place. His first order of business, he thought, was to search out his old buddy who had hooked him up with the cleaning crew job at the Embarcadero and earn some cash. His second option, which seemed like the better of the two options, was to leave the city altogether and start over.

As he walked towards a bus stop, he passed a familiar, black Mercedes coupe that was parked on Bryant Street a block away from the jail. He abruptly stopped and paused a moment, before taking several deliberate steps backward. He peered into the front of the car. Katherine sat behind the wheel. He leaned in the passenger side window.

"Is this my greeting party?"

Katherine's phone started to ring, but she ignored it.

"Get in."

They stared. He didn't move.

"It's OK."

"I believe it's best if I keep moving."

"Get in."

He studied her, then glanced around before sliding into the car. Her phone continued to ring.

"I stopped to see you recently," she said as he raised up the keychain. "You look pretty good."

"Looks don't tell the real story."

"How come no visitors?"

"It was easier that way. I didn't want to feel like I was missing the party, you know. What do the kids say? FOMO- fear of missing out."

They stared. Neither said a word for a few moments. Her phone stopped ringing. She looked away and talked into the steering wheel.

"Why didn't you tell me William took my wallet?"

"You knew he took it. And besides, I didn't want you to come to me because my brother is a heartless asshole. I wanted you to come to me because I made you feel something you've never felt before."

"I want to feel that way again, but …," she paused.

"But not enough to leave Billy."

"I'm pregnant."

There was a short silence as they studied each other.

"Congratulations. I'm sure Billy's …"

"He doesn't know," she interrupted as her phone started to ring again. "I just found out."

They both looked at the ringing phone.

"He won't stop 'til you answer."

In the distance, a speeding silver Cadillac sedan skidded into a parking spot at the entrance of the county jail. William got out of the car in a hurry, holding a phone to his ear.

"Oh, Christ," Jonathan mumbled, studying his brother from a distance.

Katherine's phone stopped ringing as William disappeared inside the building. Jonathan opened the door of the Mercedes.

"What are you doing?"

"You're here to say goodbye, right? I better go before he finds out I'm not in there anymore."

As Jonathan got out of the car, Katherine's phone started to ring again.

"You'll make a swell mom. But make him be the shadow from now on."

She glanced at the county jail parking lot. William exited the building in a rush and stood by his car, holding his phone.

"So long, Katherine."

"Don't leave."

"What?"

"Please. Don't leave. Not yet."

"I spent eight months trying to forget you."

"Get back in the car."

"Goodbye, Katherine."

Her phone continued to ring. Jonathan shook his head.

"Please."

"I can't."

Jonathan glanced back to the parking lot. William scanned the area and had spotted the Mercedes. Jonathan looked to Katherine.

"I have to go. This is about the two of you. I can't be caught in the middle."

William approached in a hurried pace.

"He's going to chase you down. You know you can't get in trouble again, especially right here in front of the jail."

With a shake of his head and after an initial hesitation, Jonathan jumped back in the Mercedes. Her phone stopped ringing.

"You better get out of here then."

William was closer as he dashed towards them. He was only 20 yards away. Katherine studied Jonathan.

"Go!" Jonathan yelled. "Let's go!"

William frantically approached. He was less than five yards away. As he desperately reached for the front passenger door with both hands, Katherine slammed her foot on the accelerator. The Mercedes squealed away, leaving William in her trail of dust, grasping at air.

Katherine kept checking the rearview mirror as she sped away. Her phone started to ring. Jonathan stared out the back window for a moment before looking back to her.

"Is he following?"

Jonathan didn't answer, only stared at her.

"Has he gotten in his car?"

Jonathan wouldn't answer. He continued to study her.

"Shouldn't he be coming after us?"

"You're making a mistake."

Katherine focused on the road in front of them. Her phone continued to ring. Jonathan again turned and glanced behind them. William was nowhere in sight. Neither of them said a word for a few miles as she recklessly pulled the Mercedes onto an exit for a busy Highway 101. She reached for the ringing phone and powered it off.

"Is this what you want?"

Ignoring Jonathan, she checked the rearview mirror and aggressively maneuvered the speeding car into the passing lane, cutting off one car, to accelerate and pass several others.

"Katherine? Please. Let's pull off the next exit," Jonathan pleaded as she continued to ignore him. "Are you sure this is what you really want?"

"Yeah," she snapped sarcastically, glaring at him, before looking back to the roadway. "This is exactly what I want. I'm pregnant, speeding, and running away from my husband. What more could a girl have."

"You can't just drive away."

She continued to focus on the road and picked up speed.

"Katherine, slow down," he continued to plead as she checked the rearview mirror again. "Slow down."

She gripped the steering wheel tighter and drove faster. The speed of the Mercedes topped 100 miles per hour.

"Come on, slow down."

"Slow down?" she asked, trading glances between Jonathan and the road. "I would think this would be fun for you."

"Jesus Christ," he mumbled. "I feel like I'm back in jail."

Neither said a word for several minutes as the car continued to speed along the expressway.

"Come on, Katherine. Slow down," he tried to reason with her. "Billy can't catch you now. It's all right."

"I need to talk with someone. Anyone."

"Then slow down."

She slowed the Mercedes and eased it out of the passing lane.

"I have no one, Jonathan."

"You got me. It's not like I can go anywhere right now. Let's talk."

"I'm terrified about becoming a mother," she confessed, glancing over to him. "I'm tired of being married. At least to William. My life has turned to shit."

"You should be telling Billy this."

"I can't talk to him," she said, looking back to the road. "He's never around. I can't even tell him I'm pregnant."

"Do you want a kid?"

"Yes, so very badly. But now ...," she said as her voice trailed off.

"But, what?"

"Now," she said, pausing. "It feels like a terrible mistake."

"What are you scared about?"

"Everything. I don't want to screw the kid up. William's been a real asshole lately."

"Come on."

"Will I be able to provide for the it? Will we bond? Will I feed it the right food? I don't know what I'm doing. I've never been around a baby."

"You have nothing to worry about."

"Will having the baby change my relationship with William?"

"Maybe that'd be a good thing," he said. "Maybe this is exactly what the two of you need right now."

"I don't know. We've been really struggling lately. I can't stand him most of the time. He can be such a pompous jerk. I don't want to bring a baby in that world."

"You'll be fine. Talk to Billy. All new mothers have the same fears."

"I can't do it alone. The thought of that overwhelms me."

"Who says you'll be alone? Where will Billy be?"

"He spends all his time at the clinic or golf course. Most of my days are spent alone. I don't want any kid to feel that. Because I know. I had a lonely childhood."

"And because of that, your kid has nothing to worry about. And you don't either."

"I don't know," she shook her head and glancing to him. "I don't trust William anymore."

"I'm sure it'll be OK," he said, not really believing his own words.

She stared to the roadway. Neither said a word for several miles.

"Have you ever thought about being a father?" she asked, changing the subject.

"Of course," he quickly answered with a grin and outstretched arms. "A few times, you know, when past girlfriends were late."

"Be serious," she said, half-smiling. "Something tells me you'd be a fun and attentive father."

"Yeah, right. Before I went to jail, I was bathing in the bathroom sink of a gas station."

There was a long pause as Katherine took the next exit off 101 and headed in the direction of downtown. She continued to trade glances with him and the road. He sensed she wanted him to say something, but he didn't know what.

"I'm going to miss you, Jonathan," she finally spoke up. "But I can't ..."

"I know," he interrupted. "But you'll be fine. Everything will work out. You'll see. What do they say? Parenting is the toughest job you'll ever love. But you need to tell Billy you're pregnant. Don't run from it."

"Where am I taking you?"

"Anywhere downtown. I need to get the motorcycle. The owner of the Tam picked it up from city impound and had it fixed."

"You going to be all right?"

"Don't worry about me. I got this bike and time. That's more than most people have."

She pulled the car to a stop at a red light. Neither said a word nor looked at each other during the stop. The light turned green, and she glanced at him.

"Will I ever see you again?" she asked.

"Who knows? Maybe in another lifetime, a long way from here."

She pulled the Mercedes through the intersection.

"Like I said, you'll make a swell mother. Everything will work out. You'll be the best mom to the greatest kid in a family everyone will envy."

"Is that all there is?"

"You never know. Maybe you'll find that it is. You can have it all, but don't let Billy hold you back."

"What are you going to do?"

"I plan to ride the bike north to Petaluma. I know someone there who tells me they can get me work at a vineyard."

"Sounds like fun."

"Sounds hard to me. I thought about staying around here, but it's probably best I get out of the city and never come back."

"Are you afraid to leave?"

"Nope," he shook his head. "I want a fresh start. I don't think I could ever get any lower than I've been here."

"What about your family?"

"I hardly see them as it is. I don't think anyone will notice I'm gone."

Katherine stopped the car at an intersection across from the Tam. He hopped out of the Mercedes.

"I'll miss you."

"I'll miss you, too," he said, staring back into the car. "You came into my life at the right time. But I have to move on."

"Please keep in touch."

"I can't. You know that."

They continued to stare.

"Be careful, Jonathan. Please."

"Don't worry about me," he said, changing the subject. "And like I told you, make Billy your shadow. Take control."

"I tried, but he'll never change."

"Don't give up," he said, motioning to her belly. "You got more to think about now."

She didn't respond, only nodded.

"If you two are meant to be together, it'll work out."

"I need a whole lot more than that."

"It'll be OK. You'll see," he said, before pausing. "So long, Katie. You changed my life."

"Don't," she said, lowering her head and trying to hold back tears.

"What?"

"Please don't call me that," she said, glancing over to him and wiping the tears from her eyes.

"I thought you liked it."

"I do, but …"

"But, what?"

"Katie feels like someone else. But not me."

"Everything will work out for you. I promise."

He smiled. She nodded and again wiped away the tears. They stared at each other until she smiled back. He then tapped his fist on the door of the Mercedes a few times without saying a word before dashing across the street. At the entrance to the bar, he hesitated before entering and looked back to Katherine one last time. She glanced away as he disappeared inside.

Katherine sat alone in her favorite coffee shop sipping hot tea. She had been there for a few hours. Her eyes were red from crying. Staring at her lifeless phone on the table, she reached for it, and powered it back on. The phone came back from the dead with a long series of beeps and buzzes. Ignoring the numerous voicemail and text notifications that suddenly appeared on the screen, she quickly thumbed in a number.

"Hey."

There was a short pause.

"I'm at the coffee shop."

There was another pause.

"Yeah, I'm all right. I know. I know. I'm alone."

There was a longer pause.

"Can you come and pick me up?"

There was a short pause.

"Thanks."

She shut off the power to the phone and waited.

Chapter Eleven
I Can't Promise You Much

The sun was quietly setting on the city and Jonathan's time there. Shades of blue and purple seamlessly mixed with the orange and red glow of the skyline at dusk. He revved the engine of the motorcycle at a stoplight. For eight months, he longed for one place. He hoped that it hadn't changed and prayed that no one else had discovered it. He couldn't get there fast enough. He didn't know after that night if he would ever be back to experience it again.

He raced the motorcycle up a backroad around a grouping of winding hills outside the city. Darkness soon engulfed him as he disappeared in the cover of overgrown pines and redwoods. He pulled the motorcycle into a clearing. Blinking lights from hundreds of fireflies flickered in the night. He shut off the headlight of the bike and gazed for a moment at the distant city skyline.

Cutting the engine, he pulled out a cigarette and lit it. Before he could get off the motorcycle, a rustling coming from behind a tree caught his attention. Katherine appeared out of the shadows. He eased himself off the bike and approached her.

"How'd you know I'd come here?"

"Where else would you go?"

"How'd you get here?"

"A friend."

They stared.

"Did you tell Billy you were pregnant?" he asked, but she didn't answer. "Did you even go home?"

She shook her head.

"He deserves to know."

"It was easier this way."

"This isn't about being easy," he said as they continued to stare. "Let me take you home."

"Not this time."

He studied her a moment. She reached for his hand and led him to a spot they had shared before. They took a seat under a pine with heavy, low hanging limbs and gazed out over the bay. Fog slowly crept over the city lights. He handed her the lit cigarette. She shook her head and motioned to her belly.

"Right," he nodded, flicking the cigarette away.

She slid her body closer to his.

"Hold me, Jonathan."

With an awkward hesitation, he wrapped his arms around her. She pressed her body deeper into his embrace. He leaned his face next to hers. She closed her eyes. Their lips softly brushed. He quickly pulled away. She opened her eyes.

"You were right," she said without expression. "No one was supposed to fall in love."

He nodded and held her tightly. She rolled her body around in his arms and was soon asleep. For several minutes, he watched. In her sleep, her stresses looked to have disappeared. Her breathing slowed and relaxed. The deep lines on her forehead and around her eyes forged by recent tensions suddenly vanished. As she slept, her phone slipped from her pocket and fell to the ground. Jonathan briefly stared at the phone before reaching for it. Trying to ease his body away from her, she awoke.

"Where are you going?"

"Nature calls," he said, secretly grabbing the phone. "I'll be right back."

She nodded as he slid away from her. He hurried to a wooded area 30 yards away and pulled out the phone, typing the letters, 'I-C-E' (In Case of an Emergency), on the keypad. The phone on the other end started to ring and was quickly answered.

"It's me, Jonathan."

He paused as William screamed on the other end.

"Calm down."

He paused.

"Calm the fuck down, Billy."

There was a longer pause as William continued to rant.

"Katherine doesn't know I'm calling you."

He paused.

"Calm down."

He again paused.

"The two of you need to talk."

He paused.

"This isn't about me. This is about you and Katherine."

He paused as William continued to yell and scream.

"You need to come and get her and bring her home."

There was a short pause as William remained silent on the other end.

"Do you remember that hillside outside the city that I once drove you to soon after I got my driver's license? We're there."

There was a short pause.

"I won't let her go anywhere."

After nearly an hour, Jonathan finally heard a car approaching. Katherine slept in his arms as they leaned against a tree. The engine's rumble and the crunch of the tires on the uneven dirt road woke Katherine as the car neared. She glanced up at Jonathan. A silver Cadillac sedan familiar to her pulled into the clearing close to where she sat with Jonathan. The car parked, leaving the engine on. She stood and stepped into the bright beams of the headlights aimed at her. She looked to Jonathan, then hesitated a moment, before walking to the idling car and getting in. Jonathan glanced to the Cadillac. William angrily glared back at him.

Jonathan pulled out a cigarette, lit it, and figured that would be the last time he would ever see her. But at least he knew, he had done the right thing for once when it came to his brother. And he didn't want Katherine to make a rushed decision that she would one day come to regret.

Katherine warily approached the car, inhaling deeply before pulling the heavy door open. Even before she could slide into the passenger seat, William angrily shouted at her. It was what she'd come to expect.

"What the fuck, Katherine? You make me drive clear out here in the middle of fucking nowhere. I don't have time for this. You know that. I must be at work early in the morning. *I am busy.*"

"If you're going to scream, I'm getting out."

"He's a nobody. You know that better than I do. Chasing after him."

She grabbed for door handle.

"This is useless," she mumbled.

He reached over and pulled her arm away from the door.

"We've been together so long, baby," he said in a calmer tone. "You're not going to throw it all away, are you? Over him? He has nothing. No prospects. No future. Nothing. You know that."

"This isn't about Jonathan. It's about us."

"He's a felon for chrissakes. You have it all. I make sure you have the nicest things."

"I can talk to him. He listens to what I have to say."

"You're set. We're set. That's why I work so hard. He'll never be able to provide for you the way I can. I will give you whatever you what."

"Maybe you can't give me what I need."

As William and Katherine argued inside the car, Jonathan leaned against a tree hidden in the woods for what seemed like forever, nearly smoking an entire pack of cigarettes. He suddenly heard the car drive away. He took the last four or five puffs on the cigarette he was smoking and tossed it to the ground.

He stepped from the wooded area into the clearing. Katherine stood alone, off in the distance, facing the fogged over city skyline. He slowly approached. She didn't turn to face him.

"What'd you tell him?"

"I didn't tell him anything. He did most of the talking," she paused, still not looking at Jonathan. "He promised me the world."

"Did you tell him you were pregnant?"

She shook her head, "I didn't want to have to fight for the baby. He would've won that, too."

She finally turned to Jonathan.

"I didn't know what love was until I met you. I didn't understand what freedom was."

"Freedom can be overrated. I know. It's been mostly loneliness and desperation."

They studied each other.

"Why'd you call William?"

"I didn't want to lose my only brother."

"So, you chose him over me?"

"No," he shook his head. "I care about you too much. I didn't want you to do something stupid. I know where I've been. I worry you may follow me there."

They studied each other a moment.

"I'm surprised he let you go so easily."

"He wasn't going to drive a motorcycle through a wall to be with me."

"I hope you know what you're doing."

"Love is running away from a million-dollar dollars."

"I lied to you earlier today," he confessed. "I told you that I wasn't afraid about …"

"Sssh," she whispered, putting a finger to his lips before he could finish. "Don't."

She moved her finger away.

"I'm frightened as hell about where I'm headed after tonight."

"Me, too," she nodded. "But for the first time in my life, I don't care."

"If you follow me," he said, before pausing, "I can't promise you much …"

She leaned in and kissed him, before he could finish.

"I can give you what you need," she said, pulling away from him.

Draped in fog, the morning came quietly. The air was calm but cool. The birds still slept in the trees. The fireflies had long burned out. Jonathan and Katherine didn't say a word as they hurriedly gathered their things as if afraid they would change their minds about running off together. They also wanted to beat William if he was on his way back for her.

Their clothes were damp from a heavy layer of dew that had fallen overnight. They couldn't look at each other. Jonathan got on the motorcycle and kickstarted it. She lingered a moment, frantically scanning the wooded area where they had slept. Finally, she joined him and crawled on the back of the rumbling bike.

"Where's my helmet?" she asked almost in a panic, her breath hanging heavy in the frosty air.

"I didn't bring it," he shrugged, glancing around the bike.

The motorcycle zoomed down the dark, empty highway. The sun had yet to rise. Jonathan raced the bike as if they were late for an important event. Katherine's arms were tightly strapped across his chest. Her long brown hair freely danced in the wind behind her. She stared into the back of his leather jacket. She looked at nothing else. He had hoped from the start she would be the one who saved him from himself. But by the end, it felt as if he instead was trying to save her. He wanted to believe he hadn't failed. And in the coming days and months ahead, he certainly needed to prove to her that she had made the right decision in leaving San Francisco with him.

As the fog thinned and the sun rose over the mountains to the east, Jonathan and Katherine cruised across the Pacific Coast Highway on the motorcycle. They headed north towards wine country. The calm ocean water glistened in the early morning light. He pulled the cable car keychain from his pocket and glanced back to her. Katherine finally looked up to him. They stared at each other without much expression. He reached the keychain out to her as it danced in the air that violently rushed around them. After an initial hesitation, she took it and squeezed it tightly. They continued to stare at each other. He slightly smiled. She never changed expression, pulling the keychain close against her chest. He peered back to the roadway ahead and gunned the bike faster as they chased after the rising sun of the new day. She rested her head on his back and tightened her hold around him. After several miles, Jonathan finally peeked to the roadway over his shoulder. Nobody followed or gave chase. The highway was empty. The fog behind them had finally lifted.

THE END